EAGLE'S PREY

Death was coming in the eye of the dawn, El Diablo thought. *And there will be fire in the sky.*

Yes, Fernando Cortes Hernandez believed he was stronger than any DEA man would ever be in a hundred lifetimes. Agents of the DEA were impotent. They were men who dreamed of a drug-free world, dreamers who wanted to believe in the job they were doing. But they couldn't touch him, because he had the money. The big money. The kind of money that God had. As long as the politicians and the police accepted a piece of the biggest action the world had ever seen, he would remain free—and he would keep on playing God.

Or the devil. He was the one with the real power. The power of life and death. . . .

Bantam Books by Dan Schmidt.
Ask your bookseller for the books you have missed.

Eagle Force # 1—CONTRACT FOR SLAUGHTER

EAGLE FORCE # 2

DEATH CAMP COLOMBIA

Dan Schmidt

BANTAM BOOKS
NEW YORK · TORONTO · LONDON · SYDNEY · AUCKLAND

DEATH CAMP COLOMBIA

A Bantam Book / October 1989

ISBN 0-553-27901-7

Published simultaneously in the United States and Canada

Bantam Books are published by Bantam Books, a division
of Bantam Doubleday Dell Publishing Group, Inc. Its trade-
mark, consisting of the words "Bantam Books" and the
portrayal of a rooster, is Registered in U.S. Patent and
Trademark Office and in other countries. Marca Registrada.
Bantam Books, 666 Fifth Avenue, New York, New York 10103.

PRINTED IN THE UNITED STATES OF AMERICA

KR   0 9 8 7 6 5 4 3 2 1

*This one's for Floyd and his Saint Patrick's juggernaut.
Together, they help keep the foursome flying.*

DEATH CAMP
COLOMBIA

Prologue

Fernando Cortes Hernandez was smiling. He had been dealt a setback, but he was back on the road to recovering his empire, and he would return to his throne, the gilded man. The smile vanishing, he rested a cheroot on his thin, bloodless lips, snapped the twenty-four-carat gold case shut, and slipped the smokeholder inside his suit jacket. With a silver Ronson lighter he torched the cheroot, then ran well-manicured fingers over the lapel of his jacket, relishing the exquisite cool touch of a thousand dollars' worth of Thai silk against his skin. He stared through the French double doors. Beyond the lagoon, he saw the first golden rays of dawn jagging across the southern Florida sky. A pelican spread its wings and flapped over the lagoon. Six Drug Enforcement Agency agents, armed with assault rifles, patrolled the grounds beyond the ivy-trellised and palm tree-fringed patio.

Death was coming in the eye of dawn, the man known as El Diablo thought, drawing the sweet cheroot smoke into his lungs. *And there will be fire in the sky.* The fire of the Devil.

Soon, El Diablo told himself, soon he would be a free man again. And the world would once more belong to him . . . and all its riches.

Death would bring him freedom. Shortly, he would get back to business as usual.

1

"Look at that guy, willya." Stiles grunted. "Christ, the sight of him makes me sick. It's all I can do to keep from ripping his throat out with my bare hands."

Short but muscular, the swarthy, dark-haired Hernandez flexed his left hand, feeling the strength flow through his veins, his blood running hot with a burning hunger to be free. He wanted to laugh at the DEA agents sitting nearby. The tall muscular agent named Stiles was losing badly at a game of spades. The shorter, heavyset Jameson chuckled each time he set his partner. Life was a game, after all, Hernandez decided. In his game, however, there were no winners—only survivors. And only one king of the mountain, one god of an empire that stretched around the world.

One conqueror.

Yes, Fernando Cortes Hernandez believed he was stronger—much, much stronger—than any straight DEA man would ever be in a hundred lifetimes. Both physically and financially those agents of the DEA were impotent, he thought. They were men who dreamed of a drug-free world, dreamers, *sí*, who wanted to believe in the job they were doing. Blinded, either by dreams, ambition, or their own smallness in a world they could never control, what they didn't want to see was that cocaine equalled big money. Big, big *dinero*. The kind of money, Hernandez thought—and he felt another tight grin stretch his lips— that God had. As long as politicians and law enforcement officers accepted a piece of the biggest action the world had ever seen, the world—and particularly *los Estados Unidos*, Fernando Cortes Hernandez knew—would never be drug-free. And he would keep on playing God.

Or the Devil. He was the one with the real power. The power of life and death.

"Relax, Big John. The Colombian's shit, we all know that. There's no sense getting your blood pressure pounding over him. I'd hate to see you have a heart attack right before the big day when we start to flush this piece of shit down the toilet. Besides," Jameson added, smiling, "you'd better get your mind back on this game of spades. At fifty cents a point, I'm up three hundred and twenty-five points."

They knew he could hear them, perhaps even wanted him to show anger over their barbs and cynical remarks. But they were as nothing to Fernando Cortes Hernandez. Indeed, they were less than the campesinos of his country. His cartel worth in excess of fifty billion dollars a year, worth far more than the 31.6-billion-dollar GNP of his own country, Hernandez knew he could buy and sell them all a thousand times over. And, if he couldn't buy and sell them like the dog meat they were, he thought, he could crush them like the worms they were.

"Look at this place, willya? A fancy mahogany bar in the corner of the room, loaded down with booze. A goddamn Jacuzzi in the living room. A stinkin' Olympic-sized pool out back. A bed with satin sheets for the drug-pushing shit. Cable television. We gotta keep the Colombian on ice in a palace that would make English royalty look like they were living in poverty."

"You know the routine, Big John," Hernandez heard Jameson say with a sigh. "We've got to keep these hotshot federal witnesses comfortable so they don't change their minds about singing. At least, that's the theory, anyway."

Hernandez kept smiling. He was used to style. And, he had to admit, the spacious, stone-and-marble mansion, secluded somewhere south of Miami, was indeed stylish. The DEA had broken their backs to make him comfortable. Then again, they had also broken their backs to extradite him from his ranch house outside of Medellín. Had he not been so burned out from four straight days of partying, the DEA men would never have caught him.

3

Rule of thumb in the cocaine trade: Never get high on your own supply. But when a man is refining close to fifty tons of cocaine a month, he could afford to dip into his own supply, Hernandez thought. Hell, he could afford to shovel into the stuff.

"Only this snowbird may be snowing us about his big plea-bargaining routine," Stiles growled. "That Federal Witness Protection tag leaves a real bad taste in my mouth. For some reason, I got the feeling our boy here may just be buying time."

"For what?"

"I dunno. How should I know?"

Jameson smiled indulgently. "Take it easy, Big John. Remember, paranoia will destroy ya."

"Paranoia, huh? We've got twenty of our people and ten Miami vice cops toting M-16s and submachine guns, assigned to protect the life of a cocaine vampire who calls himself the Devil," Stiles bitched. "And for what? So he can have his big day in a Miami court and walk away on some technicality? Plea bargain his way back to Colombia? Maybe some judge who's got a nose-candy habit himself getting bought off by those big cocaine dollars? I'm not just paranoid, guy, I'm getting blind pissed-off just thinking about how these *coquitos* can twist, bend, and shit all over the system. And nobody seems to be able to do a damn thing about it. We nabbed him, sure, but the cocaine king is far from dead. If you ask me, all this beefed-up security may just be a sore thumb looking to get hacked off. And we're that thumb. Look at 'im," he said, jaw clenched, eyes burning at Hernandez. "Federal witness, my ass. Big songbird. Bullshit."

Jameson sighed. "How many death threats have been issued against our people this last week? Death threats that have been carried out, I'll remind you. Our agents overseas have been practically under siege since our people bagged and extradited Hernandez from Colombia," Jameson said. "Three agents shotgunned to death, then hacked up in the streets of Bogotá—a street full of witnesses, but nobody saw or heard a damn thing. Four more submachine-gunned in Bolivia. An agent in Panama shipped back to DC in bits and pieces. Now the hellstorm's blowing right across our own backyard—the family of a vice cop kidnapped and tortured to death right here in Miami."

"And you can bet we've got the sonofabitch behind it all," Stiles replied. "Right here, grinning from ear to ear, in our faces. Like he knows something we don't. I tellya, either he bullshitted us about testifying, or somebody down there is scared he might start pointing fingers to save his own skin."

Blowing smoke, Hernandez turned away from the French double doors. "You have a big mouth, hombre."

"What's that?" Stiles growled, and suddenly draped his hand over the stock of his M-16. "You say something, shithead?"

"Relax, for chrissakes, will you, John?" Jameson implored. "Get your hand off that M-16 before you do something stupid."

"Stupid," Hernandez said with a chuckle, then looked away from Stiles's burning gaze. "Stupid, perhaps. Bitter, sí. Simple, sí. Yours is a simple job for a simple mind. A simple man is often a bitter man, too. Simple life. Bitter ways. Dead-end life."

"I don't see how you quite figure all that garbage about dead ends, Hernandez," Stiles said, his voice edged with anger. "You're the one who got caught with your lips locked on a crack pipe and dragged out of Colombia."

"The world," Hernandez said, solemnly gazing at the guards near the patio, "is a whore, and you must indulge her. The sooner you learn that . . . the better off you'll be."

5

Stiles grinned at Jameson. "The world's a whore? Now what's that—"

Suddenly, the DEA agents froze, locked gazes. The cards slipped out of Stiles's hand.

The throbbing seemed to descend right on top of the safe house.

"Are we expecting company?" Stiles rasped, snatching up his M-16. "That's a chopper! Nobody told me anything—"

The sounds of autofire and screams lanced through the windows of the room.

Looking skyward, Hernandez smiled, his eyes lit with grim anticipation. He flicked his cheroot aside as the French Aerospatiale Alouette swooped from the murky sky. A split-second later, as the DEA agents opened up on the converted gunship with a barrage of M-16 autofire, the chopper turned the stygian gloom ablaze.

Fire ripped the dawn sky asunder.

A glowing tongue of white phosphorous fire spewed from the long nozzle on the gunship's nose. Shrieks ripped the air and M-16s went silent as the DEA agents burst into human torches. Flaming demons crashed through the trellis, wrapped in slick-looking sheets of fire. A wave of flames consumed the patio, devouring plant and human life alike.

A demon danced in front of the French double doors. Flailing, he tumbled through those doors, wailing like a banshee. Glass shards razored past Hernandez, who held his ground. Silently, he dared the fickle gods of fate to hurt him.

"Jesus Christ!" Stiles gasped, freezing in his tracks for a second, his face cut with horror and shock as the blood-curdling screams filled the room. "We're being hit! What the hell's—"

Hernandez then saw the dark shadows pouring out of

the woods. Automatic weapons chattered in their fists, spewing hot lead over the stunned DEA agents.

"You sonofabitch! You planned this whole thing! You set us up!"

Hernandez whirled. There was murderous rage in Stiles's eyes. For a moment, the cocaine czar would have sworn that Stiles was going to cut him down in cold blood.

"John! John!"

The demon's screams died. The stench of roasting flesh pierced Hernandez's nose. It was a good smell, he thought. The cleansing fire. The corpse was the charred, shriveled symbol of the moral decay of the United States.

Then Hernandez saw the pencil-tip flame spitting from the muzzle of Jameson's M-16.

Stiles cried out, a line of 5.56mm slugs marching up the backs of his legs. As Stiles crumpled to the floor, Hernandez scooped up the fallen M-16. For a stretched second, Hernandez and Jameson stared at each other.

Teeth gnashed, Stiles grabbed at his legs, rolling around in a growing puddle of his own blood.

Hernandez smiled at Jameson. The furious din of autofire crushed in on the safe house.

"So I am a piece of *mierda,* eh, hombre?"

Jameson shrugged, appearing apologetic. "C'mon, give me a break. I had to make it sound convincing."

"No . . . no." Stiles looked up at Jameson, his eyes burning with hatred. "Not you. Not—"

"Finish him, hombre."

Regret flashed through Jameson's eyes. He looked down at Stiles. "Sorry, Big John. What can I tell you? I got caught in a tangled web."

Without hesitation, Jameson drilled a three-round burst into Stiles's chest.

The gunship lowered to the ground beyond the shattered French double doors. Rotor wash hurled chips of glass against Hernandez. His gaze narrowed against the glass shrapnel, Hernandez told Jameson, "Your information had better be good, hombre. Or you will not live to see the sun set. *Comprende?*"

The smoking M-16 lowered by Jameson's side. "It's good. I wouldn't risk my ass like this if it weren't."

Hernandez grunted.

There was a commotion behind Jameson.

Three swarthy men surged through the doorway. With long strides, Hernandez moved toward his soldiers. They toted Argentine FMK-3 submachine guns. Hernandez smiled. There was no mistaking his *segundo* and top assassin, Raul "El Leon" Pizarro. Six and a half feet tall, with shoulder length hair as black as coal and an eyepatch over his left eye, Pizarro, Hernandez knew, could put fear into the heart of the toughest of hombres. There was a huge machete sheathed in black leather at Pizarro's side. More than once, Hernandez had seen El Leon hack the arms or legs off an enemy and feed the bloody stumps to a caiman.

"Fernando," Pizarro said in greeting, and the two men hugged each other. "I knew we would see each other again."

"Once again, Raul, you have shown you have the courage of a lion."

"They were nothing. The place is surrounded. All of the DEA men are dead. Another helicopter is on the way now to lift us out."

"Good, good. We must leave now. Quickly."

Suspiciously, Pizarro looked at Jameson. "Wait a minute, Fernando. What about him?"

"Him? Do not forget—that gringo has the master list, Raul. He lives . . . for now." A cruel smile then stretched the cocaine czar's lips as he looked at the body of Stiles. "Let us see, though, if he has the stomach for what may lay ahead in the days to come for his DEA amigos. Give our new addition to the New Conquistadors your machete, Raul."

Jameson tensed as Pizarro slid the machete from its sheath. "Wh-what . . ."

"Be quick about it, hombre," Hernandez snapped at Jameson. "Raul, you watch him and make sure he does admirable work. If he hesitates, kill him. Sometimes they vomit over such work. Should he vomit, kill him."

Jameson looked at the machete as if it were some contagious virus.

"Take it!" Hernandez barked.

Trembling, Jameson took the machete. "Wh-what . . . what do you want me to do with it?"

Hernandez smiled. "You are to make Big John not so big, hombre, that's what."

El Diablo laughed.

It was back to business as usual.

Chapter 1

The statistics were frightening.

The newspaper headlines were horrifying.

The world had gone mad.

Vic Gabriel felt his teeth set on edge. Expelling a pent-up breath, he looked up from the *Washington Post*. Beneath Gabriel was a glaring headline about the massacre of DEA agents and Miami vice detectives at a safe house in Dade County, a hit that had gone down because of the extradition of a drug baron from Colombia. Another major supplier of cocaine, who had also been extradited recently from Colombia, had been quoted in the article Gabriel had just read: *"Cocaine will be the atom bomb that destroys the United States."*

The sonofabitch had that right, Gabriel thought, and felt the bitterness eating away at his guts.

Cocaine had killed his younger brother, Jim, years ago.

Following his brother's death, Vic had launched a short but explosive war against the death pushers, up and down the East Coast. During that war, Gabriel had formed a close ally within the Drug Enforcement Administration. That agent, Bob Jeffreys, had sympathized with Gabriel and put his job, and his life, on the line for Gabriel in the belief that fire had to be fought with fire. For days now, Gabriel had been poring over and mentally chewing up the intelligence Jeffreys had air-expressed to him from across the Atlantic Ocean. The statistics were enough to send someone reeling in disbelief. More than two billion dollars of cocaine was squeezed into Florida alone every week. And that, according to the agent's intel, was a conservative estimate . . . a very conservative estimate. It was reported that only one in every nine hauls of cocaine was seized by law enforcement officials. Tons of cocaine were stockpiled in refineries in Colombia, Bolivia, Peru, and other South American countries. Plenty of the black snow, Gabriel thought, to replace any load that was confiscated. The DEA and other law enforcement agencies simply didn't have the manpower or the money to win the war against the *narcotraficantes*. It was the drug barons who had all the money, all the manpower. And they never hesitated to flex muscle when and wherever necessary to get what they wanted.

Shaking a Marlboro free from a rumpled pack, Gabriel flicked a gold-plated Zippo, torched the smoke. Engraved on the Zippo was 7TH SFG—NO COMPROMISE. The Zippo was a memento from his father, Colonel Charles Gabriel who had helped in the conception of the Special Forces in 1952.

Vic Gabriel himself was ex-Special Forces. He was also a former assassin for the CIA's Special Operations Division. It was because of the CIA that Vic Gabriel and the other three commandos of Eagle Force were forced to set up a new base of operations in the Pyrenees along the French-Spanish border. Eagle Force's last mission, a killhunt against the Soviet SPETSNAZ up the icy slopes of Mount Makalu in Nepal, had also locked them in the death sights of a CIA execution squad. After that mission, Eagle Force had wiped out the rest of that Company hit team in the Florida Everglades. Used as expendables by the CIA for a mission that had resulted in failure in Nepal, Eagle Force knew that the CIA would never give up the hunt to terminate them now. With the large sum of money they had managed to stash in a Swiss bank account after their first mission, the commandos of Eagle Force had bought out and set up their war base in a chateau high up in the Pyrenees. Like any number of the ten thousand other chateaus in France, Gabriel's war base was originally built back in the Dark Ages to protect landowners from the barbarian hordes of Franks, Visigoths, and Burgundians. Vic Gabriel found grim irony in that. He knew there was really no safe place, no protection anywhere in the world from the savage hordes of animal man.

Which was why Vic Gabriel had originally formed Eagle Force. Law enforcement officials and the military could only do so much. Governments were handcuffed by international laws and treaties, and their obvious inability to stem the tide of terrorism and narcotics trafficking had only thrown gasoline on the fire. The civilized world had been put on the defensive by terrorists and international criminals who were launching the offensive in their hunger to take and consume what was not theirs, in their evil ambition to impose their will on the rest of the world. More than once, Vic Gabriel had felt the sting of the terrorist viper. His father had been murdered by terrorists in Paris. His father's murder had also been the poison of CIA treachery.

Pushing himself away from the long oak knights' table, Vic Gabriel scraped the legs of the straight-back chair over the stone floor. Standing, he walked away from the knights' table. As he moved toward the stained-glass windows, washed in the sunlight that knifed into the briefing room, he glanced at the frescoed murals. Alexander the Great and his Greek and Persian legions battling the Indian prince Porus and his war elephants. Hannibal, the Carthaginian general, crossing the Alps with elephants to march into Italy. Frederick Barbarossa, the German emperor of the Holy Roman Empire, accepting the surrender of Henry the Lion, Duke of Saxony and Bavaria. The Allied Forces hitting the beach at Normandy under heavy Nazi fire. Napoleon and his Grande Armee retreating from a Moscow wrapped in a mountain of flames. The carnage at Gettysburg. The Prussians saving the day at Waterloo.

A student of history, Vic Gabriel knew that, as a warrior himself, there were important lessons to be learned from battles long since won and lost. Lessons to be learned from man's triumphs . . . and from his fatal mistakes.

And now one of the worst cancers the world had ever seen was eating away at the guts of the free world.

Cocaine.

Opening up the stained-glass windows, Gabriel stared at the view beyond the chateau. It was early morning, and a low bank of clouds, like giant cottonballs, cloaked the jagged peaks and rocky slopes of the Pyrenees massif. Gabriel let the sunlight warm his face. Far below the walled courtyard, Gabriel spotted a wild goat, perched on a ledge, staring, it seemed, off into infinity.

Even though his heart was hurting with memories of the past, even though his mind was searching for answers to stem, or at least disrupt, the tide of narcotics trafficking into his country of birth, Vic Gabriel enjoyed the cold air he sucked into his lungs. It was good to breathe clean air.

The ex-Special Forces warrior heard the massive oak double doors open behind him. Turning, he watched as the other three commandos of Eagle Force walked into the briefing room.

The white-haired, granite-faced Zac Dillinger led the troops toward the knight's table. Torching a fat Cuban cigar with a Zippo, Dillinger glanced at his Seiko. "Zero-eight-hundred on the dot, V.G. You said it was urgent.

14

Christ, I hope so," he cracked good-naturedly. "This old war dog isn't used to crawling out of the fartsack at this ungodly hour."

Gabriel closed the stained-glass windows.

"It wouldn't have something to do with this creep from Colombia, would it, Vic?"

Gabriel saw Johnny Simms—the black ex-merc who had done a free-lance stint down in Central America and had nearly lost his life at the hands of a sadistic commandante— tack the face and computer printout of Fernando Hernandez to the team's WANTED: DEAD billboard. The billboard was another one of Gabriel's personal touches in the briefing room. On the billboard the faces, histories and crimes of every major terrorist and narcotics kingpin read like a Who's Who of the underworld. They were the targets.

And Eagle Force did the manhunting.

"A bloody cocaine warlord. Fernando El Diablo Hernandez," gruffed Henry Van Boolewarke, the ex-Recce commando. "Christ's eyes! According to that printout, the Devil has more money than Exxon and half the Third World countries combined. And an army of killers that rule Colombia, to frigging boot—with the help of the authorities they have tucked securely in their pockets, of course. Yeah, I've read it, and it makes my blood boil to think these shits can get away with murdering whole innocent families of decent law-abiding officials because they're got more money than Christ Jesus in Heaven."

"Is El Diablo up for removal, that the next program, V.G.?" Dillinger, the ex-P.I. from sunny Fort Lauderdale, wanted to know. "We going after the Colombian connection?"

"Take a chair. I'll make this brief short, but it'll be anything but sweet."

Eagle Force sat at the knights' table.

Gabriel moved to the head of the knights' table, puffing on his Marlboro. Okay, he thought, the immediate answer to the war on drugs was right there in the briefing room. After one hellfire mission together, Gabriel knew that Eagle Force had become a four-man juggernaut that could roll over any enemy, anywhere. Of course, no enemy anywhere would just lay down and watch his empire crumble into ashes and ruin.

"I've got four tickets to get us en route for Miami International tomorrow," Gabriel began. "Now, I take it you've read the printout on El Diablo and his so-called New Conquistadors?"

"Yeah, Vic, we've read," Simms answered, "and I've got to tell you, this is a large order to fill—if you're thinking about going after the Devil himself, that is."

"There's no *thinking* about it, Johnny," Gabriel said. "I don't care how well organized the New Conquistador cartel is, or how many corrupt officials they've got in their pockets, or how big their army of killers is. The United States and her allies have got a knife pressed right against their throats. My source inside the DEA sent me a three-hundred-page report on the cocaine plague . . . and I don't think I have to tell you that they're fighting a losing battle."

"You got that right, V.G." Dillinger said, chomping on his stogie. "The coquitos are worth tens of billions. With the kind of money they're worth, those assholes can buy and sell entire countries."

"Can?" Boolewarke echoed. "Try *have*. Cocaine trafficking runs whole countries. Look at Panama. Honduras, the Bahamas, Haiti. And Cuba, too—Ivan's even gotten into the big cocaine action. Ivan won't have to drop the bomb. Hell, no. He'll just wait until everyone's burned out on cocaine and march right in with a few fat keys. The high's on Mother Russia, boys and girls. Have a hit, burn the flag, and bend over and let Ivan drive it to you."

The bitter anger in Boolewarke's voice didn't escape

Gabriel. Years ago, the Afrikaaner had been ambushed in Angola by a SPETSNAZ murder squad. Because he'd been hunting a notorious SPETSNAZ major-general in that southwest African Marxist hellhole while under contract to the CIA, Gabriel had been able to save the Dutchman and his Recces squad from certain slaughter. One by one, with a high-powered rifle, Gabriel had sent those Russian-Cuban goons reeling into the bush and across the blood-stained dirt of Angola. The Dutchman wasn't one to forget favors. Which was one of the reasons Boolewarke had originally joined Eagle Force—after his ranch in the Transvaal had been razed by fire and bullets by African Nation Congress guerrillas. Briefly, Gabriel recalled the black day he'd found Boolewarke, a shell of a man, crouched over the bullet-riddled carcass of his pet lion, Thor. Hatred of communism drove Boolewarke. Hatred of Marxist lies and deceit. Militant communism had shattered Boolewarke's life. With nothing to lose, the Dutchman went into every battle, both guns blazing...never looking back. The Dutchman just preferred to go toe-to-toe with Ivan or his cronies.

Hell, none of them had anything to lose by fighting international criminals their own way, Gabriel reflected. Johnny Simms had been a pool hustler and backstreet fighter, down to his last dollar and out of luck when Gabriel and Dillinger had hauled him out of a biker bar in Virginia Beach.

Zac Dillinger had been a private investigator with a lust for strip-joint dancers that had probably cost him two marriages. Even though old Zachary, Gabriel thought, would never admit he'd done anything to deserve such misfortune at the hands of such gold-digging sluts. Like he really had any money to begin with. Alimony, mounting unpaid bills, and IRS trouble. No question about it, Gabriel knew, Dillinger's freebooting, ass-kicking ways had landed him on the Death Row of straight society living.

Only they were all mavericks unable to fit into straight society living. Perhaps what really separated all of them from that daily ax-and-grind of straight society was a fire in the belly. A desire to try to really do something to keep chaos and corruption from plunging the world into an abyss from which it would never emerge.

"All right," Gabriel said, "we're meeting my man in Florida tomorrow night. He's rounded up the key intelligence on Hernandez and his New Conquistadors, so he'll steer us in the right direction. We're going after the newest, biggest, and obviously deadliest of the Colombian cocaine cartels—the New Conquistadors. Any other questions, I'll fill you in on the drive to Paris."

Simms looked confused. "That's it?"

"That's it, for now. It's search and destroy, all the way."

"What, is the DEA paying the tab on this one?" Dillinger asked, blowing a thick cloud of cigar smoke across the table.

"Is that all you think about, old man? Money?" Boolewarke growled.

"Hey, listen, after setting this chateau up the way we wanted, after buying up almost a hundred grand worth of computer equipment," Dillinger shot back, "and since our Swiss bank accounts are down to the low five figures, yeah, I think money's a legitimate concern, damn right."

"Nobody's paying us on this one," Gabriel informed his commandos, his voice firm with conviction. "This one's for free. But if you want a fee, we can work something out. It'll come out of my pocket, you have my word."

Eagle Force stared at Gabriel with questions in their eyes.

"I don't understand, Vic," Dillinger said. "Is there something here you're not telling us?"

Gabriel knew that none of them were aware of his brother's death by cocaine. But he wasn't in the mood to tell them. He was geared up to roll.

"Listen, my reasons are personal," the ex-CIA assassin said, his gaze steely. "I've got a real chip on my shoulder where druglords and their middlemen and street pushers are concerned. They're vipers. Scum. Parasites. I want them crushed. We're headed in the direction of Bogotá, or wherever the trail leads us to in Colombia, that much I can tell you. How we'll get there, how we'll eventually tackle this mission, I can't tell you for certain. I just know we're going to make some noise. Some real loud, ugly noise."

Hard silence filled the briefing room.

Dillinger blew smoke, the gray cloud curling over the carnage at Waterloo. "Hell, V.G., that's good enough for me. South France is starting to bug me anyway. I've been itching for some action for weeks now."

Gabriel looked away from his commandos. He felt the fire in his belly. Pay or no pay, Gabriel saw the fire in their eyes, too.

Eagle Force was ready to spread its wings again.

And the Devil be damned.

Chapter 2

According to the captain, Flight 665 was less than two hours out of Miami International. Where Eagle Force was headed, and what they were up against, Vic Gabriel thought that it should have been tagged Flight 666: the mark of the beast.

The flight of the devil, to be damn sure.

Eagle Force was about to wage war against the Cocaine Hydra. Once again, the veterans of countless killing fields were hurling themselves into the fire.

Staring out the window in the first-class cabin, Gabriel watched the shadows of twilight stretching over the infinite expanse of the Atlantic Ocean. In the distance he saw the sun, suspended like a giant fiery orange-red eye on the rim of the horizon.

Bad Zac Dillinger sat beside Gabriel, and Simms and Boolewarke sat across the aisle. Boolewarke was sleeping and Simms was boning up on the DEA report on cocaine trafficking. Gabriel had lost count of how many Bloody Marys Dillinger had consumed during the flight, but every time the flight attendant came by to take a drink order the ex-CIA assassin could count on Bad Zac to try a new *coffee, tea, or me* line on the busty stewardess. Where good-looking women were concerned, Bad Zac never gave up the hunt to get one in the sack. The ex-P.I. had a long track record of uncontrolled libido that had gotten him into more than one jam.

"You've hardly said two words the whole flight, V.G. Can I ask what's bugging you? Gut feeling's telling me there's more to this mission than you've let on, old buddy. Let it out. It might help to talk about it. What's going on with you, huh?"

Gabriel heard Dillinger, but the ex-P.I.'s voice seemed to come from a mile away.

Gabriel ignored him. Lost in the darkness of the past, he went back. . . .

Back to the genesis of that private war. . . .

Back to Death. . . .

A wide ivory grin cut the black face. "We don't know no Jim Gabriel, motherfucker. But I tell ya what ya can do for us. Turn over your cash, honky, and we'll forget we had this conversation. Now that sounds like a deal to me. Cold cash will save your white ass."

They laughed.

There were two of them. He had staked the dealers out, followed them to one of their crack houses in Fort Lauderdale. Less than a hour ago, Vic Gabriel had forcibly fed a pusher an ounce of the potent cocaine derivative, crack, torturing information out of the scum that would help him find his younger brother, Jim. The pusher claimed that Jim got his "shit" from a couple of "dudes" called Mo and Skeebo. Gabriel had also gotten the address to their crack house before the pusher died from cocaine intoxication. The whole time his system was being poisoned with his own stash, the pusher had whined that Gabriel had to get him to a hospital to have his stomach pumped.

"You played, pal," Gabriel had told the crack dealer. "Now you're paying the price. That crack, pusher man, ain't all it's cracked up to be."

Gabriel had left that guy to drown in his own poison. In Gabriel's mind, when a guy lived like shit, that's how he ended up. Every man got what he deserved.

And some got what they didn't deserve.

It had been a long, tough week of caving in doors and kicking the hell out of dope dealers in South Florida.

Now Gabriel stood alone in a dark alley, staring down two switchblades. Gabriel just wanted some information that would lead him to his brother. But the hoodlums obviously thought they might be able to take a little cash off him to help feed their crack habit, Gabriel thought.

Gabriel was hunting. And he was in the mood to disappoint his enemies. He wasn't about to feed anybody's drug habit.

Just indulge their death wish.

Gabriel held his arms out by his side. "I'll tell you what. If you can take it off me . . . you can have it. That's the deal, girls."

The hoodlums looked at each other, appeared set to laugh.

"Why, you white motherfucker—"

Their attack was uncoordinated. The switchblades swept for Gabriel's throat, one after the other. Instead of circling wide in their attack and hemming him in, the hoodlums rushed Gabriel, thinking they had an easy kill, driven by their own mindless rage over the insult. Even if their attack had some semblance of lethal coordination and skill, it would have done the hoodlums no good. Gabriel had been trained to kill. Quickly. Quietly. Efficiently.

When the hoodlums missed slashing Gabriel's face into raw hamburger with their initial attack, they left themselves wide open for a counterstrike. A split second was all Gabriel needed to end the confrontation. Like a bolt of lightning, the ex-Special Forces warrior struck.

One hoodlum found his balls crushed to mush and floating around somewhere in his lower intestines.

The other hoodlum had his nose bone driven up into his brain by the tip of Gabriel's elbow.

As switchblades clattered to the asphalt, Gabriel fisted a handful of the surviving hoodlum's Afro.

"Now maybe we can talk like civilized men, Mo, or Skeebo, or whatever you're calling yourself, asshole," Gabriel rasped through clenched teeth. "Spill your guts, or spill your guts. Not much of a choice, but that's the deal."

The hoodlum clutched at his punished crotch, gasping for air. "Hey, m-man, easy, easy, you're fuckin' crazy! Man, you must be on some strong shit! Ahh! Easy on the 'fro, bro. Shit, I think I know the dude you want. Jim Gabriel, right?"

"Right."

"They call him Jimbo, Slim Jimbo."

"Are we talking about the same guy? White guy?"

"Yeah, yeah. Shee-it, he even looks kinda like you, man. Same eyes. Same build. We shoot 'im the crack. Bulk, man, bulk. The dude was movin' big bulk for us, but the motherfucker's fronted out where we's concerned. He owes, and he's gonna get fucked up bad if he don't stop smokin' up the whole load and pay back what he owes the Big Man. Jimbo's got a smoke habit that's cutting into the Man's profit, and the Man don't like that. The boy's itchin' to get fucked up."

"You're going to get fucked up if you don't give me an address."

The hoodlum gave Gabriel an address in Pompano.

"Thanks, asshole. And by the way," Gabriel growled, pinning the hoodlum with graveyard eyes. "You're all fronted out, too."

And Gabriel smashed the hoodlum's skull into the

cold concrete of that alley with one stomp of his paratrooper's bootheel.

The address led Gabriel to a swank beachfront condominium high-rise in Pompano. It came as no surprise to Gabriel that his younger brother was living in style and luxury. Selling dope was easy money. Hustling cocaine was both big and easy money. And his brother, Vic knew, had always sought the path of least resistance.

Since childhood days, when both of them had been raised on a ranch in the Colorado Rockies by the Colonel, Vic had spotted the seed of self-destruction in his brother. Where Vic had pushed himself to the limit, both physically and academically, his brother was always a word away from throwing in the towel. Where Vic listened and obeyed his father in order to become something better, his brother rebelled and became something less in his disrespect and ignorance. Was character then, Vic often wondered, something an individual was born with, or something acquired through struggle, through trial and error? Whichever, the brothers had grown apart.

One went to fight in the Vietnam War.

The other one fled to Canada to smoke pot and organize underground protest movements.

The opposite ends of the spectrum were now on a collision course.

Wondering what he would say or do to his brother when he saw him, Gabriel rode the elevator to the twentieth floor of the high-rise. This wasn't the first time he'd confronted his brother about the hell he was making of his life. Though he'd never used illegal drugs himself, Vic Gabriel had been around long enough to see just what a dead end drug abuse was. He'd seen firsthand what opium addiction had done to the average grunt in Vietnam. Addicts were inevitably sapped of energy, with only the desire to do nothing but chase their next high. For a soldier, that could well prove fatal. For the civilian, where there was a will there was a way when running down that next hit. Robbery. Deceit, Murder, too. Drug addiction came with a huge price tag attached to it. It stole money. It carved the heart, the nucleus out of whole families. It ruined jobs, ended careers. It killed.

Even though his brother would never be a soldier, Vic Gabriel had always hoped that Jim would at least remember some of his father's wisdom. And, no, a warrior wasn't necessarily someone who went to battle to fight and kill the enemy, their father had said. Rather, a warrior was a man who went to great lengths to do what was right, respect others, and live by a code of honor and decency, even when the world around him was doing its damnedest to go to hell. A warrior could well be a man who raises a family, loves his wife, and struggles with the trials of day-to-day living. A warrior could damn well be the average guy who went out the door in the morning to tackle the day, and end that day knowing he had given it one hundred percent . . . and then some.

Drug addiction robbed a man of character.

Gabriel knocked on the door to his brother's condo. Then he heard the weak sobs beyond the door. Alarm bells sounding in his head, Gabriel found the door unlocked.

Stepping into the living room of the condo, he found himself entering a nightmare.

The young blond girl was cradling Jim's head in her arms. Consumed by grief, she was unaware that Vic was standing over her.

Taking one look at his brother, Gabriel knew right away what had happened to Jim. Rage overpowered his sense of bitter frustration and helplessness.

The rubber strap, like some obscene noose, was still wrapped around Jim's arm. To Gabriel's eyes, the needle seemed to grow out of that arm like . . .

A grave marker.

The condo was decorated with expensive, fancy furniture, but Gabriel saw only the glass coffee table. On that table were two crack pipes, several rocks of crack cocaine, and a propane torch.

The first time Gabriel had learned about his brother's involvement in cocaine, Jim had told him, "Maybe you'd lighten up a little bit, big brother, if you took a hit off the pipe. It might make you feel better about life. Maybe even about yourself and other people, instead of walking around like some hardass who's gotta fight the whole world. You oughta relax and you might enjoy life a little, big brother. It's gonna kill us all, anyway."

"Why would I want to do that?"

"Do what?"

"Take a hit."

"Let me tell you, Vic, there ain't nothin', *nothin'* in the world like that fifteen-second burst of euphoria when you're hitting that pipe. Not sex. Not all the parties and all the good times you've ever had. Nothin', man, I mean nothin'."

And nothing was what his brother had been chasing all of his life, Vic Gabriel saw, and felt the tears burning into the corners of his eyes as he stared into Jim's vacant gaze. Or just what had he been chasing, Vic Gabriel wondered? What had driven his brother to this horror? Why? Was he himself responsible in some way for his brother's death? Could he have helped prevent this? What could he have done? How could he have been there for his brother?

But his brother had been nowhere, and *nowhere* was exactly where Gabriel realized he would have fit in Jim's life.

Nowhere was dead.

The girl finally looked up at Gabriel. Trembling, she

stared at him for long moments, as if trying to compre-
hend his presence there. "I told him . . . I told him not to
fire the shit. Mainlining will kill you, if you don't know
what you're doing. One air bubble . . . just one. I told
him . . . I told him. He fired a whole gram. God! It was
them, I know it was them. The pressure, the worry. He
was scared. Jesus, he knew they were coming . . . he
knew . . . he was in deep, way over his head."

"Who? Who's *they*?"

The girl buried Jim's face in her bosom. "One air
bubble . . . one lousy air bubble . . ."

One air bubble . . . one lousy air bubble . . .

"Vic! Vic! Snap out of it. What the hell are you
muttering about?"

"What?"

Startled, Gabriel stared at Dillinger. It was only then,
as he looked at Dillinger, Simms, and Boolewarke, that he
realized he'd been talking out loud.

"Man, Vic, what is eating you?"

There was genuine concern in Simms's voice. Debat-
ing whether or not to tell the commandos about his
brother, Gabriel focused sudden impulsive anger on Dillinger.
Looking up from the Bloody Mary in Dillinger's hand,
Gabriel growled, "You're cut off, or you can go back.
We've got a mission. We're not going to some goddamned
party, playboy. This is serious business, read me?"

Dillinger looked stunned. "Yeah, sure, Vic, sure.
You're right."

Several seconds of uneasy silence passed. Gabriel
stared out the window.

Finally, Gabriel looked at Dillinger, "Sorry Zac, forget
it. I've got a lot on my mind. Go ahead and have another
one."

"Like I said, old man," the ex-P.I. told Gabriel. "If you want to talk about it—"

Gabriel looked away from his commandos, a haunted expression shadowing his face. "There's nothing to talk about. What's done is done. My brother... I was just thinking about him."

"I didn't even know you had a brother, Vic," Dillinger said. "You've never talked about him."

Gabriel let it out, point-blank.

"That's because he's dead. I found him with a needle in his arm. He was a cocaine addict."

Dillinger just looked at Gabriel.

The ex-Special Forces warrior stared back out the window, squinting into the sun. All right; now they understood.

It was personal.

Chapter 3

Vic Gabriel felt his blood boil as he read the dossier on the New Conquistadors.

"*I have seen the Devil. He is me. And he is you. And he is everyone around you.*' Now what the hell's that supposed to mean?" Vic Gabriel asked ex-DEA agent Bob Jeffreys as he looked up from the dossier, the dim overhead light burning down on the mug shot of Fernando Cortes Hernandez, illuminating the swarthy face and laughing eyes of the coquito in a pale, ghostly hue.

Jeffreys, a big, broad-shouldered man with a crew cut and a salt-and-pepper mustache, dressed in a gray windbreaker and black slacks, steered the Chevy van north on A1A. Palm trees, looming like sentinels in the night, lined the sidewalks along the stretch of intercoastal highway leading into Fort Lauderdale. Beachfront hotels lined the strip and bars were congested with beer-swilling college kids.

There would be no party for the commandos of Eagle Force.

Eagle Force was moving toward their first battle front.

The Chevy van was an arsenal on wheels.

The commandos of Eagle Force sat on a bench behind Gabriel. At the moment, they were checking the weapons Jeffreys had acquired for them.

"Who knows? El Diablo's always spouting off at the mouth with some strange words of warped wisdom," Jeffreys growled. "One of my favorites is *the world's a whore*. Now you figure that one, coming as it is from the whoremaster himself. Whatever, their only motivation seems to be love of the almighty dollar."

"Poets and philosophers they ain't," Simms gruffed, slapping a thirty-round magazine into a compact Ingram M10 SMG. "Scumbags peddling human misery and death in the name of pleasure, they are. I was born and raised on the mean streets of the nation's capital. The bagman rules there. Always has. But it's gotten worse, a lot worse. From what I've seen on a couple of trips home, and from what I've heard on the news lately, the streets of DC are under siege by pushers killing each other and innocent bystanders from the crack trade. Ten-year-old kids are hustling crack and getting killed in the crossfire of the bigger dealers. Some life, huh? Washington, DC, is now called the crack capital of the country, thanks to dudes like Hernandez." Simms shook his head. "Values, my man, their values have somehow gotten all screwed up. You gotta wonder who is really to blame. The kids? The parents? Teachers? Government? Who? These kids see so-called sports heroes making millions a year and pissing it all away on nose candy . . . it makes you wonder about values, or lack of."

Dressed in combat black like Gabriel and Simms, Boolewarke and Dillinger screwed silencers to their own Ingram SMGs. As they had for the previous two missions, the Dutchman and the ex-P.I. toted their favored weapons. Riding quickdraw leather on his hip, Dillinger carried the Colt .45 automatics, the pearl-handled butts of his Blood and Guts specials jutting forward for a crossdraw, and the bulge in Bad Zac's pants pocket betrayed the presence of his brass knuckles. Leaning beside Boolewarke was his Barnett Panzer crossbow, a weapon the Dutchman had proven himself to be lethal with and could boast one-hundred-percent efficiency. Ka-Bar commando knives were also sheathed in black leather on the hips of the commandos in case their first hit called for silent kills. Vic Gabriel's own Ingram SMG with attached silencer rested on the floorboard beside him. The former CIA assassin intended to make their presence in South Florida felt— hard and bloody. Gabriel intended to bag a big coquito and use that kingpin to somehow, some way get them inside the Colombian drug world. Events, Gabriel knew, and violent confrontation would dictate the terms of his strategy.

"And like anything else, it'll get worse before it gets better," Gabriel said.

"If it *ever* gets any better," Dillinger added. "Seems like the cops clean out one area, arrest a hundred dealers, and another hundred crop up out of nowhere. The dealers and would-be dealers are like leeches falling out of the frigging sky! And now we're after some lunatic who believes every man is the Devil and the world's a whore. Christ!"

"I'm not even going to try to get into their twisted minds," Jeffreys said, "or slap you in the face with the staggering numbers law enforcement officials are up against...."

"Like the fact that Americans spend more than a hundred fifty billion dollars a year on illegal drugs," Boolewarke cut in.

"Not *spend—waste*," Dillinger added, firing up one of his Cuban stogies with a flick of his Zippo. "Hell, that's money users oughta just put a match to."

"So you see what the law's up against," Jeffreys continued. "Of course, the administration's whole point is that if there's no demand, there's no supply. That's never been the way I've seen it. Cut off the supply, there's no demand. There had to be a supply for there to be a demand in the first damn place."

"Now they're talking about legalizing narcotics," Simms said. "But look what happened with alcohol in this country after Prohibition. Shit, you make cocaine legal, well, I'd hate to get on a plane with a pilot who's burned out from a four-day coke binge, more worried about his next line than landing that plane safely."

Jeffreys shook his head. "Legalizing dope sure isn't the answer. In my view, that'll only make the problem worse."

"What about the military?" Dillinger asked. "What about pinning down the spots where they're growing the coca leaf and spraying the stuff from the air? I understand the coca leaf is primarily grown in Peru and Bolivia. It shouldn't be hard to pinpoint the trouble source and give the areas a good clean aerial sanitizing."

"No good," Jeffreys answered. "The DEA's hashed that one over, too. You see, the thugs already have that angle covered in their pursuit of megabucks and megapower. Now they grow legitimate crops near the dope fields, usually in inaccessible places in the jungle."

"The result," Gabriel said, "is that you kill bean plants and other legitimate crops, plus you start killing off the jungle, and the next thing you know the government's crying greenhouse effect. Talk about a vicious cycle."

"That's one of the reasons why I quit the DEA, Vic," Jeffreys said, his voice edged with disgust. "It's a losing battle because nobody really wants it won. Sure, there's all that big talk by politicians now about the war on drugs that has to be waged if we're to save democracy from the drug thugs. Talk's about all it is, pal. Too many of the people who are in positions to do something to stop the flow of drugs are taking fat kickbacks to keep the *narcotraficantes* in business. I've seen literally tons of cocaine virtually disappear from under my nose after a big bust, and nobody knows the first thing about it." Jeffreys laughed bitterly. "So, if the law's dirty..."

"You can't give up the fight, though," Gabriel said in a somber voice. "No problem is that insurmountable. You've just got to get to the head of the Hydra. Lop it off in all-out battle. That's why we're here."

Jeffreys gave Gabriel a grim smile. "I never quit, Vic, and I'll never give up the fight, either. I've got children myself, and I'll be damned if I'll see their lives torn apart by drugs. Quit? Never. Why the hell do you think I fed you the intel I did and steered you in the right direction during your own private crusade? Just like I'm doing now."

Gabriel wasn't questioning Jeffreys's resolve; he was merely talking out loud, wondering if maybe the real powers-that-be felt the war on drugs was, indeed, a hopeless battle. Suddenly he noticed Jeffreys looking into his sideview and rearview mirrors for the third time in as many minutes. Checking his own side mirror, Gabriel spotted the dark blue four-door sedan, one block down.

"A tail?" Gabriel asked.

"What's the matter?" Dillinger wanted to know, a cloud of dark smoke pinned beneath the ceiling above him, the ex-P.I. flicking ashes on the floorboard of the van.

"There were two of them," Jeffreys informed Eagle Force. "The other one peeled off about a half-mile back. Damn it! We've got trouble. Turn the page, Vic, and you'll see your boy here in South Florida, and I'll explain what my gut feeling's telling me is up and coming."

Warning bells began to sound in Gabriel's head. Traffic was sparse on A1A at 0210. The beaches were practically deserted, but several couples strolled the sidewalks and walked along the beach, hand in hand. Gabriel had no intention of mixing it up with whatever enemy was

33

dogging them. A running gun battle down A1A would bring the local law down on them like a hurricane. And Gabriel wasn't a warrior to put innocent bystanders in the middle of flying lead. But somebody, Gabriel was certain, was on to them. Or after Bob Jeffreys.

And, no, the enemy never gave a damn about innocent bystanders.

Thumbing through the dossier, Gabriel rested his gaze on a long-haired, ferret-faced guy with a goatee. An ugly grin slit Gabriel's lips. "Ramon Falconi. Alias the Falcon. Alias Johnny Lightning?"

Jeffreys chuckled, but there was no mirth in the sound. "El Diablo's main distributor here in South Florida. Also known as El Halcon, the Falcon, Johnny Lightning, and maybe a dozen other pet nicknames. He owns entire banks down in Panama and the Bahamas, where he launders his dirty billions. He's believed to be moving in excess of ten tons of cocaine a month into the States, and once again that's another conservative estimate. Now, I've been staking Johnny Lightning's operation out for a week, trying to pick up his routes, his drops, delivery points. I'd have to say, judging by our tail, that I've been made. Bet your buns Lightning's our ticket to the coquitos and all the kingpins to the south."

"*Our* ticket?" Gabriel questioned, looking Jeffreys dead in the eye.

"Hey, ole buddy, you didn't think I was just along for the ride, didya? I put my butt on the firing line to get you this intelligence on the New Conquistadors and Johnny Lightning. You wanna clip the Falcon's wings, I'm here for the clipping."

"Forget it, Bob. You've got a wife and kids, and they need you a lot more than we do. This is a solo act for us, all the way. Hit and run. Search and destroy. You've done your part. I'd just as soon drop you off at Pier 66 and let you drown your worries in a pitcher of cold beer."

Jeffreys appeared to think hard about what Gabriel said for a long moment. "Right, guy, but you may change your mind about my involvement once you find out what you're up against."

Gabriel grunted but let the ex-DEA man's persistence fall on deaf ears for the time being.

"First of all," Jeffreys went on, "you've got to get to Johnny Lightning. You'll need transportation down to Colombia and the Falcon's got an international computer business, his front, that deals with Japan and most countries in Western Europe. Meaning the Falcon's got enough private jets and helicopters—your transportation, if you can commandeer one of his birds—at an airfield south of Miami to move an army. And an army is exactly what he commands. An army of killers and sadistic thugs—just like El Diablo has. The coquitos are all interconnected and protected—within and without the law.

"Which brings me to another point. During the past two months several DEA agents in South America and officials high up in the Colombian political scheme of things have mysteriously disappeared. The operative word there should be *kidnapped*. A special DEA task force, working under deep cover inside Colombia, went on a hunting excursion into the jungle. They'd gotten a lead about the disappearances of the targeted people from a source in Bogotá. Unfortunately, only one agent made it back out of the jungle to tell his tale. And he had a bullet in his gut by the time the DEA was ready to exfiltrate him. It would appear," Jeffreys said, glancing at Gabriel with somber eyes, "that El Diablo is running some kind of death camp in the Colombian jungle."

"A death camp?" Gabriel echoed. "What purpose

would it serve to kidnap, torture, and kill the people he's trying to convert to his twisted way of thinking?"

Jeffreys shrugged and looked into his sideview mirror again. "Brainwashing by extortion, bribery, and murder, I would gather. They're telling these people to play ball because there's no spot on the bench for dead weight or opposition. Instead of a body count of politicos and officers in the Colombian military, they'd rather have allies they can count on when the heat comes down from Uncle Sam. But the way things are going down there, Colombia's about a year away from the lawlessness of Lebanon. Once that happens, Uncle Sam won't be able to touch it, and all the extradition treaties in the world won't mean squat. Now, what I want to know is how you plan to tackle the New Conquistadors. You know about the massacre that freed Hernandez here a few days ago, so you can see these people are serious. Dead serious."

"So are we," Boolewarke said.

"So am I, friend," Jeffreys growled, catching the Dutchman's eye in the rearview mirror. "That slaughter that freed Hernandez cost me some lifetime friends. I was with the DEA for fifteen years, and I know an inside job when I see one. The minute El Diablo started that bullshit about plea bargaining I knew something bad was going to go down. And it did."

"What about these New Conquistadors, Bob?" Gabriel asked. "I thought the Medellín cartel controlled most of the world's cocaine?"

"They do. The thing is, the Medellín cartel has gotten huge—so huge that they've outgrown themselves in terms of money and power. These kingpins have sons and relatives, it's all part of a family business, much like the Mafia here at home. Apparently, the Medellín cartel was looking to expand. Now they're moving tons of cocaine across the Atlantic to Europe. The Brits seized a thirty-ton load last month—of almost pure cocaine. Now they're saying there's a new form of cocaine, more powerful and more addictive than crack. The Colombians are already using it, and it's only a matter of time before it hits the States. We're sitting right on a time bomb, and my experience in the DEA is warning me that there should be a lot more people in power running scared over this shit than there are. It's all getting bigger . . . and deadlier. And it's spreading like wildfire."

"So in steps the New Conquistadors," Gabriel mused. "Worldwide expansion."

"Right," Jeffreys agreed, "and if Western Europe goes the way the United States has gone . . ."

"Ivan would have a field day right in his own backyard," Boolewarke finished. "Provided, of course, the shit doesn't cross over the Berlin Wall."

Jeffreys stared through the windshield, his gaze riveted on something ahead. "Oh-oh. Looks like we just found that missing sedan. Showtime, people."

Two blocks ahead, Gabriel spotted the sedan. Another four-door sedan pulled out of a side street, shot across the south- and northbound lanes, and braked to a stop, sitting like a barricade in front of the Chevy van. That sedan carried four shadows. Gunmen.

"I'd have to say we're being hit, V.G.," Dillinger pointed out, grinding the cigar beneath his bootheel on the floorboard.

"And I've got the rear guard coming up hard!" Gabriel rasped, the sedan growing in his sideview mirror. "Pull it off the highway, Bob. Take 'em down by the water. I don't think these guys care too much about the local civilian populace."

Simms cocked the bolt on his SMG. "Looks like surf's up, fellas."

"A bloody crimson surf," the Dutchman added, "at high tide."

A split second later, the small windows in the back of the van were punched in by a lead firestorm. Boolewarke, Simms, and Dillinger ducked, bullets thudding into the back doors.

Teeth gritted as glass chips razored through the van. Gabriel saw the pencil-tip flames stabbing the darkness in his side mirror.

Cursing, a Colt Python revolver filling his fist, Jeffreys sent the van bounding over the sidewalk, the right front fender clipping a palm tree.

"Looks like I'm involved now, Gabe," the ex-DEA man growled, "whether you want me or not."

"Get ready to pile out!" Gabriel ordered, snatching up his Ingram SMG. "If you can, save us a prisoner."

"If we can, we will, Victor!" Boolewarke shouted as lead continued to pound into the back doors of the van. "Right now, I'd like to save my own ass! You might have to take a rain check on a broken promise!"

The Falcon, Gabriel thought. *Let me clip your wings, you bastard.*

Broken promise or not, Gabriel was going Falcon hunting.

Then, slugs screaming off the hull of the van, Gabriel saw the sideview mirror disappear in an explosion of glass and metal strips.

The Falcon's predators were swooping for the kill.

Chapter 4

When he was an assassin for the CIA's Special Operations Division, Vic Gabriel had been known as the Angel of Death. The title had been no misnomer. Believing that the weak needed a strong ally in the universal struggle against tyranny, he had shot brutal military dictators in Africa and the Caribbean with a high-powered rifle from two hundred yards. Despising international criminals who had no respect for human life, he had cut the throats of terrorists in North Africa and Beirut, felt their blood run, hot and sticky, down his hands. Knowing from grim first-hand experience that the Russian military and its puppet regimes were hard at work to undermine the West, he had garroted KGB agents in Bulgaria and East Germany in the darkest shadows of some forgotten European alley. It had been a job, sure, but it never hurt for a man to believe in right and wrong, to be able to separate the wheat from the chaff.

Death had been both an ally and a vicious enemy to Gabriel.

Death had taken him around the world, thrown him into countless arenas where there were no winners, only survivors. Even though Gabriel could separate the savage from the savager, Death had no conscience. And Death could just as easily savage him.

The international narcotics traffickers were no different from any enemy in Gabriel's past. They bled the world dry in their desires, devoured life in their hunger for power and glory, but were never sated. Never.

Now, as moonlight glittered off the black waters of the Atlantic Ocean like slivers of ice, the Chevy van racing toward the surf on that stretch of Fort Lauderdale beach, Gabriel found himself once more calling on his own guardian Angel of Death to guide and protect them through the firefight.

A grim realist, Gabriel knew that winners, and survivors, made their own luck. It never hurt, he believed, to call on a little divine intervention.

Both sedans were rolling up hard on the Chevy van. With the van's tires grabbing at sand, Bob Jeffreys suddenly whiplashed the vehicle into a hard turn to the left. Gabriel thought it was a crazy maneuver, perhaps even suicidal, because Jeffreys left himself exposed to the murderous lead hellstorm. Jeffreys was a gutsy bastard, Gabriel thought, always had been, but now the guy seemed to have some death wish. Gabriel only wanted for Jeffreys to live through the foray and return home to his family in one piece. *God help the Falcon's predators if something happens to Jeffreys.*

Silenced Ingram SMG cocked and ready for action, Johnny Simms slid the side door wide as Jeffreys hit the brakes, the wheels sliding through water-softened sand.

Gabriel burst through the door. Running, boots splashing water as the surf crashed against the beach behind him, the ex-Special Forces warrior angled away from the van. Teeth gritted in savage fury, Gabriel drew target acquisition on the lead sedan. Revolvers cannoned and automatic weapons flamed through the windows of both sedans. Craning himself out the back window on the driver's side, one goon was triggering an Uzi submachine gun over the roof of the trailing sedan. At the moment, Gabriel didn't give a damn if he bagged a prisoner or not, lead whining off the van beside him and churning up the sand around him. It was survival time.

Swiftly, Simms, Boolewarke, and Dillinger disembarked from the van, triggering their subguns as soon as combat boots hit the sand, the lead sedan roaring into their field of fire.

Dropping into a combat crouch, Jeffreys fired his Colt Python in a two-handed grip, 158-grain hollowpoint slugs booming toward targets downrange.

And Eagle Force unleashed a tidal wave of .45 ACP slugs on the rampaging enemy.

Glass imploded on the goons in the lead sedan. Moonlight shining dully off the hood of that sedan, Gabriel saw the face and skull of the driver erupt in a podburst of gore and muck. That sedan became a hearse as the four commandos of Eagle Force pounded the car with sizzling lead hornets. Four more gunmen were ravaged by the Eagle Force .45 ACP firestorm. Gabriel glimpsed the enemies' expressions of agony and horror as slugs chewed apart their throats, then erased their faces in a crimson wash that sucked the life right out of their black souls.

Slugs raking the sand, Johnny Simms and Henry van Boolewarke hit the sand on their sides and rolled away from the tracking lines of fire. With lightning speed, all four Eagle Force commandos cracked home fresh clips into their Ingrams.

Unmanned, the lead sedan rammed into the van. Glass exploded and metal rended, the van driven closer toward the lapping waves.

It was then, out of the corner of his eye, that Gabriel saw Jeffreys laid out in the sand. Fear for Jeffreys's condition cut through Gabriel, then return fire clawed the air around him.

The second sedan charged the four shadows on the beach like an enraged bull.

Simms dove out of the way of the speeding sedan. Fiery fingers stabbed through the front and back windows of that car as gunners tracked the rolling figure of the black ex-merc with autofire. The gunman firing over the roof was kicked away from the sedan as Boolewarke shattered his skull with a three-round burst.

Kneeling, Zac Dillinger squeezed off a long burst from his Ingram, .45 ACP slugs coughing from the silenced muzzle of his subgun. Two gunmen, desperately trying to spread Simms's blood and guts across the sand, were hammered away from the windows by the ex-P.I.'s stuttering subgun. Dillinger emptied the Ingram M10's clip, flung the subgun aside, and unleathered both .45 Colt automatics in a smooth crossdraw. Defying death, pinned in the glare of the sedan's headlights for an instant, Bad Zac triggered the Blood and Guts specials. He punched in the windshield with two hollowpoint rounds, saw the driver's head explode on the receiving end of his furious offensive fire. As Gabriel, Simms, and Boolewarke marched bullets up the hood of the sedan, the white-haired, granite-faced Dillinger flung himself to the side. The sedan rocketed past Dillinger, smothering the ex-P.I. beneath a stinging blanket of grit.

As furious and as unrelenting as their counterattack had been, the Eagle Force blitz left a lone survivor.

The front passenger door to the sedan was shoved open. A figure clutching an M-16 toppled from the car and hammered to the sand.

The sedan shot past Gabriel like a bullet.

Coming out of his roll, the goon pivoted, drawing down on Dillinger with his M-16.

Gabriel, the Angel of Death, became a demon of relative mercy. Knowing he had to have a prisoner to lead him to Johnny Lightning, he beat his commandos to the draw, squeezing off a three-round burst that ripped open the goon's arm. Crying out, the goon reeled to the sand, M-16 whirling through the darkness.

The second sedan rolled into the surf. Bouncing against the surf for an instant, moonlight glimmering off the car, the sedan began to float on the gentle swells of the Atlantic.

A cool breeze brushing off the Atlantic and striking him in the face, the smell of salty air and blood in his nose, Gabriel rushed to Jeffreys's side. Rage tore through him.

Dark shadows, fused in the glow of moonlight beaming over them, Boolewarke and Dillinger reached the wounded goon first. The goon scrabbled through the sand, reaching for his M-16.

"Not so fast, pal," Bad Zac Dillinger rasped, then stomped down on the goon's shattered arm.

A shrill cry ripped the air.

"Charity's the only thing keeping you in the land of the living, buddy," Dillinger told the goon. "Don't push your luck."

Gabriel knelt beside Bob Jeffreys. Blood pumped from several holes in the ex-DEA man's chest and stomach.

Crimson spilling from his mouth, Jeffreys looked up at Gabriel through glazed eyes. He forced a half-smile, then groaned. "G-guess . . . who's gonna tell . . . the wife and kids . . . Gabe . . . if it's true . . . the good . . . die young . . . I'll never . . . make it . . . to be . . . a grandfather . . ."

"Easy, Bob, easy."

But even as Gabriel tried to comfort Jeffreys, he knew the guy was seconds away from checking out into the Great Void. Damn. Gabriel thought about Jeffreys's wife and children for a second. Sure, his wife and children would know he died in the line of duty, but that would bring little consolation to a grieving widow and children who would go through the rest of their lives without a father. Particularly since the ex-DEA man had gone renegade in a way, hunting the savages on his own terms. But was there ever any other way? Gabriel felt like pinning some of the blame for Jeffreys's suffering on himself. But he knew Bob Jeffreys the man. And even in his last breath on earth, Jeffreys wouldn't hear of Gabriel beating his head against the wall for something that was beyond anybody's control.

Or was anything ever beyond anybody's control? Gabriel wondered. Like the drug epidemic.

Like senseless violence and brutality.

Eagle Force, Gabriel knew, had just stepped over the lines and into a world that seemed beyond anybody's control. The Falcon, the New Conquistadors, he vowed to himself, were going to pay for what they'd done to Bob Jeffreys. Pay in blood dues.

"Hey, Vic, what do you want to do with this guy?" Dillinger called out. As the ex-P.I. rested a cigar on his lower lip, he asked, "Is he our ticket to fly to the Falcon?"

Gabriel looked into Jeffreys's eyes. The ex-DEA man's mouth fell open, and he struggled to say something. Then the air rasped out of Jeffreys's mouth, and Gabriel saw the emptiness fill the ex-DEA man's stare. Dead.

Dillinger flicked his Zippo, fired up his cigar.

Jaw clenched, Gabriel stood. With long strides, he moved across the sand. A full moon beaming down on his back, Gabriel stood over the wounded enemy, a dark silhouette, a ghostly figure. With terror and pain etched into his face, the goon stared up at Gabriel. It was obvious to Gabriel that the creep knew he was in deep, way over his head. Gabriel decided to play out the drama.

Suddenly, Gabriel's Ingram erupted, slugs burping from the silenced muzzle.

The goon flinched, slugs stitching the sand beside his head. There was defiant hatred in his eyes as he looked at Gabriel.

"Start sweating, pal, because your minutes are numbered," Gabriel said.

The goon spat. "Go fuck yourself."

In the distance, Gabriel heard the sirens. The lights of Fort Lauderdale along A1A burned in the periphery of his vision.

"You don't get me to the Falcon," Gabriel said, tight-lipped, aiming the Ingram SMG at the goon's face. "No face job in the world will piece your mug back together. And I won't use this Ingram, either. He is one of the Falcon's lackeys, isn't he?" he asked his commandos, as an afterthought.

Dillinger shrugged, then stepped on the goon's injured arm. "You a Falcon lackey?"

Strangling the scream in his throat, the goon showed Dillinger hate-filled eyes. "You'll never touch Johnny Lighning. Never. His world's a little too big and a little too tough for you four assholes."

Bending, Gabriel fisted a handful of the guy's shirt-front, snatched him to his feet.

"Johnny Lightning doesn't have a world, pal. He lives in a toilet bowl," Gabriel growled through gritted teeth.

Vic Gabriel was silent. Deadly silent.

Behind the Angel of Death, the sedan bobbed on the ocean swells.

Johnny "the Falcon" Lightning believed he was the man with the Midas touch. At least, he recalled, that was

45

what one of his main distributors had told him long ago. The Midas touch. Yeah, it made him feel like some god to know that every deal he made turned to gold. In his business, money was the bottom line, even though he relished the feeling of power he held over hardcore cocaine users. More than once that distributor had told him the Greek myth about King Midas, but Johnny Lightning didn't care too much for the part about the king turning his own food to gold. And Johnny Lightning often wondered if there wasn't some deeper meaning in that myth, and that maybe, just maybe, the distributor was even trying to warn him about something. But warn him about what? That a man could have too much gold? Too many women? Too much cocaine? What? Hell, Johnny Lightning loved gold, but he wasn't prepared to starve to death over it. He wasn't even that crazy about cocaine, even though it supported his gold fix in big style and flash. No matter where he went, Johnny Lightning wore gold on his fingers, around his neck, even on two of his toes. Big twenty-four-carat pieces, straight from the mines of South Africa. No, you can't eat gold, he thought, sitting in his hot tub at his private health spa, but it sure looks good on the right man. The ladies loved gold, too. They also loved Johnny Lightning and his endless supply of coke.

And Johnny Lightning liked to glitter when he was moving and shaking about town. He saw himself as the sun source of all physical pleasure. The Falcon. Right. He was like a bird of prey, he thought, swooping down to snatch in every last dime from a world gone mad. It didn't bother Johnny Lightning that he was contributing to the madness; indeed, he encouraged it. What he didn't want to encourage was the naked brunette, Sandy, snorting up a half-gram or more each time she dived into the mirror with the rolled-up thousand-dollar bill stuck up her nose.

On that mirror Lightning had dumped more than an ounce of pure ground-up coke. The way Sandy was hitting the stuff, pulling the coke up into her brain like a vacuum, Johnny Lightning knew she was getting a little too involved with that ounce. Which meant she wouldn't want sex later.

"Take it easy on that shit, willya babe?" the Falcon told her, his gaze running over her large, firm breasts that hung like melons just above the swirling water.

"Easy, easy," Sandy bitched. "Listen, if you don't want me to touch it, don't put it out, all right, Johnny? If it's here, I'm going to do it, you should know that by now."

Anger flared into Lightning's eyes. "Hey, bitch, you know how much dope I throw away on you every night? The last month alone, you've blown through a whole key, and so far I've gotten very little return for my investment, if you know what I mean."

Sandy laid the thousand-dollar bill down, sank up to her neck in the water. "Sorry, Johnny." She laughed nervously, draped her arms around the Falcon's neck, and kissed him full on the mouth. "You're right. I'll take it easy."

"That's better. Besides, at the rate you're going you'll burn a hole in your nose the size of a quarter. You wouldn't look so damn foxy walking around town with a bandage over that beautiful nose of yours, now, wouldya? Stick to the champagne for a while. Just relax, all right? Let Johnny Lightning do the walking and talking."

Johnny Lightning poured himself a glass from the imported bottle of five-hundred-dollar French champagne. He came to the hot tub room every night to relax for an hour or so, get away from the pressures of business. The coke trade had skyrocketed profits for him so much during the past year that everybody in town, from the women to rival dealers to vice detectives, wanted a piece of him—or a piece of the action. Sometimes it was hard to distinguish who wanted him from those who wanted him six feet under. The cops he could handle, because he could buy them. The rival dealers he could take care of if they stepped out of line, because he could have them shot. It was the women he had trouble with. Why was it that every lady he became involved with was a cokehead, it seemed? If Sandy starting freebasing or mainlining, she was down the road, Johnny Lightning decided. *Talk about putting a dent in the profits.* He had clients who had a million-dollar-a-year freebasing habit. He sometimes wondered if the money was worth the aggravation. Then he glimpsed the gold on his fingers, glittering in his eyes. Glittering, right, just like his life. It was worth the aggravation, and then some.

"Johnny. It's Mariani. Looks like we got another problem with our West Palm party boy."

The Falcon looked toward the all-glass bar in the corner of the room. Bruno stood behind the bar. The big, dark-haired enforcer was dressed in black silk shorts, his muscles bulging through a white double-knit sport shirt. Bruno was pouring himself a shot of bourbon, his other ham-sized hand wrapped around the receiver of the telephone to muffle his voice. Bruno carried a stainless steel .44 AutoMag in a shoulder holster.

Sighing, the Falcon looked at his reflection in the mirror beside the hot tube. He had sharp features, and the ladies often referred to his looks as "devilishly handsome." Johnny Lightning was proud of the way he looked.

Gaze narrowing, the Falcon looked at Bruno. "Don't tell me he's short . . . again."

"Yup. Six grand this week."

"Goddammit! Godfuckingdammit! You find out what the fuck's going on up there, Bruno. I shoot that asshole five bricks a week and every week now for the past month he's come up short. Right now, he's in the hole twenty grand."

"Twenty-five," Bruno corrected, glancing down at a notepad.

"Jee-zus Christ. You tell him I'm not paying for his habit or his girlfriend's habit. Plus he's been known to front keys to a couple of unreliables and I've warned him about that. The bullshit's gotta stop, 'cause he's burying me and if he buries me— I got a business to run. I got stuff that's got to get moved. And I got people to answer to myself. If all my distributors were coming up short like him I'd be floating up on Miami Beach in no time—in fucking bit and pieces. The Colombians want their money. And I want mine by next Friday, or I'm sending somebody up there. I don't care how he gets it, if he has to sell his sister, or he's got to steal it from his mother. I want my fuckin' money. You tell him that. You tell him I don't need him; he needs me. He fuckin' acts like I don't need the money, like I can give the shit away for free. You explain to him, Bruno, explain about profits, and about cutting losses."

"Right, boss."

Even though he treated his people first class, gave them expensive gifts and sometimes cash, Johnny Lightning didn't want anybody to take him lightly. His money was good. And his word was worth gold in the business. Distributors fucking around with profits weren't worth gold. They weren't worth anything but a bullet in the brain.

Bruno nodded and moved to the front of the bar, drink in hand. He started to talk into the phone when the door behind Johnny Lightning burst open. Lightning saw the fear and surprise widen Bruno's eyes, then his enforcer clawed for leather

They were being hit.

49

And, like a supernova, Johnny Lightning's world exploded before his eyes.

Autofire blistered the air, and Bruno's white sport shirt turned red.

Red with big ragged holes. Bullet holes.

Panic gripped Johnny Lightning.

He saw his life flashing before his eyes.

In red.

Chapter 5

Gabriel drove the enforcer down the length of the bar with a long burst from his silenced Ingram. The guy danced a jig of death, and the .44 AutoMag fell from his hand, bounced off the carpet. Blood streaked the glass front of the bar, and the enforcer crumpled in a heap next to his fallen shotglass. Behind Gabriel, Boolewarke, his Barnett Panzer crossbow in hand and loaded with a broadhead arrow, guarded the doorway. Simms and Dillinger, fisting their Ingram M10s, reached Johnny Lightning first.

The brunette was screaming, and Dillinger backhanded her across the mouth. "Women," he growled. "How come they always start screaming when the shit hits the fan?"

"You ain't some kinda male chauvinist pig, are ya, Bad One?" Simms cracked.

"You bet, Johnny boy. The worst."

Ramon Falconi started to jump out of the hot tub. But the kingpin bird of prey became the prey. Gabriel fisted a handful of the druglord's hair, jammed the Ingram's muzzle in the guy's face.

"Wh-what the fuck! Who the fuck . . ."

Ramon Falconi froze when he stared into a pair of eyes that glittered like chips of ice. Eyes that had seen death and violence . . . lots of violence.

Having forced the information about the Falcon's whereabouts out of their prisoner on the beach, Gabriel had then shot the goon in the head and dumped him in a garbage bin behind a bar along A1A. Garbage, Gabriel had figured, was what the guy was. The guy had sold his soul long ago, and he'd ended up right where he belonged.

Eagle Force had then penetrated Johnny Lightning's health spa in Boca Raton. With commando daggers and with the killpower of Boolewarke's crossbow, they had left behind a trail of five dead cocaine cowboys in the hallway leading to the hot tub room. As deep as they were in now, Gabriel knew Johnny Lightning was up to his neck in trouble. And if the Falcon didn't cooperate, the Angel of Death would just as soon shoot him and leave him in the hot tub to float in his own blood. He was taking the jag and the sting out of Johnny's lightning.

"I understand you've got your own private airport, Johnny," Gabriel began. He glanced at all the gold decorating the druglord and saw the guy even wore a gold band around his black Speedos. The Falcon was all flash, Gabriel decided, and found himself despising Ramon Falconi. Simms was dead-on right. The Johnny Lightnings, the big-time cocaine kingpins, peddled misery and death in the guise of pleasure. They appeared to have it all. Money. Power. Women. The good life. What was that saying? Gabriel wondered. *Living well is the best revenge.* Yeah, that was it. Well, the joke was on Falconi. His borrowed time was borrowed up.

Johnny Lightning struggled, splashed Gabriel. Gabriel dunked the druglord underwater, held him there for several seconds, then pulled him up. Johnny Lightning gagged, cursed.

"Sit tight, honey, we'll be gone in a minute," Gabriel told the woman out of the corner of his mouth.

"What the fuck you want?" the Falcon demanded.

Gabriel twisted on Falconi's hair, felt a twinge of

pleasure when he saw the druglord grimace. "El Diablo, that's what I want."

The Falcon stared up at Gabriel as if he were a madman. "You're crazy," he said with a laugh.

"And determined, too. I want you to phone ahead to that airfield, have a fly-boy in a plane, preferably a Lear. I want it fueled and ready to head out. I also want five parachutes, stuffed and ready to open. I'll be checking those chutes personally, and you'll be wearing any one of them that looks tampered with. We're southbound, Johnny. Going to the land of the coca leaf. We're taking a trip to Colombia. And we're not going there for coffee, either, pal."

Falconi was defiant. "You *are* nuts. Forget it. I ain't doing shit for you, cowboy."

"Bad choice of words, Johnny," Gabriel said, and held the Falcon underwater. Five, ten, fifteen seconds. Johnny Lightning struggled desperately, his hands clawing at Gabriel's arms. Playtime was over, Gabriel decided. Gabriel was primed for action. In one swift motion, he shoved the Falcon to the bottom of the hot tub, pinned him there with a bootheel against his throat. Finally Gabriel reached down and hauled Johnny Lightning out of the water, flung him against the edge of the hot tub. He jammed the muzzle of his Ingram beneath the Falcon's chin as he gagged and spat out water.

"One last chance, Johnny," Gabriel warned the Falcon. "I've got a tight timetable. One last time with a pretty please. Do we fly or not? With or without you, we're going. If you go, you're along for the ride . . . and maybe I'll loan you a little more time."

The Falcon appeared to think hard about something for a long moment. "Awright, awright," he sputtered, hacking up water and bile. "I . . . I don't know who the fuck you guys are, but if you're thinking about strong-arming me into taking you down to Colombia—"

Gabriel pinned the Falcon with graveyard eyes. "There's no thinking about it, Johnny. You're in this with us, all the way, till death do us part. The days of the fat bank accounts and the endless nights of partying are all over for you. You're taking us to El Diablo."

The Falcon laughed, but the laughter was strained with fear. "Sure, sure. I'll be taking you to *your* death, asshole. When El Diablo and his people get through with you, there won't be enough left of you to feed to a caiman. Ya hear me?"

Teeth gritted in savage fury, Gabriel hauled Johnny Lightning out of the hot tub by his hair. Johnny Lightning howled in pain.

"Yeah, I hear ya. But I'm not listening," the Angel of Death told the druglord.

Gabriel was concerned. There was no set strategy to the mission, and as a veteran of countless search-and-destroy operations, he was grimly aware that hit-and-run tactics would only get them so far. Sooner or later, Eagle Force would hit a stone wall of gunmen that would far outnumber the four of them. They would have to. The New Conquistadors were well armed and well organized. The Falcon seemed aware of this, too. At the moment, as Johnny Simms sat behind the wheel of the bullet-riddled but still operational Chevy van, Henry van Boolewarke riding shotgun and Zac Dillinger puffing on a cigar, Johnny Lightning began gloating over this fact.

"How far do you heroes think you'll get once you're inside Colombia, huh? You got any fucking idea at all about what you're up against? I know you're not DEA, or even CIA or any kind of feds, for that matter. Can't be. You know why? I'll tell you why, hotshit. You got some guts, I'll give you that much, more guts than those guys, but you're short on brains this week, friend. The feds are all show and no go, long on brains and small on balls. The DEA or the CIA would never fuck with the New Conquistadors like you cowboys. Those guys are nothing but pseudo-heroes in white hats. Over the years I've been in the business, I've watched those people learn hard lessons, a lesson you're going to learn, too. You see, every time somebody wanted to take a poke at El Diablo or extradite him from Colombia, something real baaaaad happened to them. Like it did right here in town just this week. You know what I'm talking about, don't you? What was it? Something like two dozen feds fried and hacked up like butchered meat." He laughed. "Wake up. There's a huge demand in this country for cocaine, and even the big shots are taking a piece of the action. Cocaine is here to stay, and there's not a damn fucking thing you can do about it. So why don't you be smart, huh? Let me out, and we'll call it even. I'll forget I ever laid eyes on you."

"For a guy who wears black, gold-trimmed Speedos," Dillinger said, blowing smoke at the Falcon, "you talk a pretty tough game, hombre."

Falconi, who was now dressed in gray slacks and a brown leather jacket, growled, "That's 'cause I got the muscle to back it up."

Gabriel looked away from Johnny Lightning. For some reason, sitting there in the presence of a *narcotraficante* like Johnny Lightning, the ex-Special Forces warrior felt the spectre of his brother in that van. It was estimated that for every 150 pounds of cocaine smuggled into the United States there was one cocaine-related death. There were a lot of Jim Gabriels out there, he thought, with their name written on a brick of coke. Maybe the drug epidemic was just another sign of the times they lived in, but Gabriel wasn't about to buy into that. If his brother was still alive, if he could be sitting right there in that van next to Johnny Lightning and see how smug and arrogant, how indifferent he was to everything but his own desires, maybe, just maybe, his brother might have taken a little harder look at himself. And maybe his brother might still be alive. Maybe. But Gabriel doubted that.

"I got a sign comin' up for that airfield, Vic," Simms announced. "One mile and ticking down to takeoff."

"You don't think our boy Lightning here," Dillinger said, "would've warned his people at the airfield through some coded message, do ya, V.G.?"

"That special envoy bit," the Dutchman added, "didn't sound very convincing to me. An envoy requesting parachutes and a special hush-hush flight plan to Colombia, to boot."

"And we look about as Colombian as Frank Sinatra," Simms put in.

Gabriel picked up the AutoMag he'd taken off the enforcer he'd shot in the hot tub room. He let Johnny Lightning take a good hard look at the stainless steel hand cannon, then hooked the .44 AutoMag inside his belt, below his kidney. Dillinger and Boolewarke had also stripped M-16s and Uzi submachine guns from the dead goons on the beach and in the spa. Eagle Force was loaded down with plenty of firepower to tackle the next battlefront.

"That jet better be ready to go, Falconi," Gabriel warned the druglord. "You'd better not be jacking us around."

"You amaze me in a way, cowboy."

"How's that, Falconi?" Gabriel asked.

A half-smile twisted Falconi's lips. "With your big ideals, you've blinded yourself to certain facts."

Gabriel found himself becoming increasingly irritated with the druglord's smugness. "What facts?"

"Like the fact that guys like me and Hernandez are

seen as modern-day Robin Hoods. Do you know how much coke money is dumped into real estate, construction, and what you call legitimate businesses? El Diablo has built entire villages for the campesinos in his country. He's feeding the poor more than just the coca leaf. He's given hope to people who had none. Myself? I've bolstered the entire real estate business here in South Florida and provided jobs for people who would otherwise be standing in line for a welfare check."

"Robin Hood," Boolewarke scoffed. "I like that, I really do. The real thing with guys like you, Falconi, is that you don't want to work for an honest living."

"I've got a multimillion-dollar computer business, wiseguy. I'm all over the world, and my company employs thousands of workers. I pay my taxes on time. I set up and supervise many deals in the computer business personally. I'm up at five o'clock every day and don't go to bed until after midnight. I'm developing a new company in Japan right now and I'm employing another couple of thousand workers. Tell me about work."

"He's right, Falconi, and you're wrong," Gabriel injected. "You don't want to work for a living because you think you're better than everybody else. Cut the bullshit; we didn't just fall out of the sky from Mars. The computer racket's just a front. Rationalize it any way you want, but the bottom line is that you're a two-bit hustler."

Anger burned in Falconi's eyes. "Coming from common mercenaries, that's like throwing stones at a glass house, wouldn't you say? That's what you are, isn't it? Common killers-for-hire. Only I'd like to know who hired you."

"We're self-employed, snowman, kinda like you," Dillinger said.

"But there's a difference, a big difference, between you and us, Falconi," Gabriel said. "Like night and day."

"Yeah? What?"

Gabriel shook his head. "Forget it. You'd never understand in a million years."

Gabriel felt Simms turning the van left. Looking through the windshield, he saw the lights along the runway in the distance. They were moving down a paved road, engulfed in darkness, flanked by trees.

"Stop the van, Johnny. Dutch, Zac, pile out. If we're walking into a trap . . ."

"I gotcha, V.G.," the ex-P.I. said.

Dillinger and Boolewarke, who toted the Barnett Panzer crossbow, jumped out of the van.

Falconi was silent, and Gabriel's combat senses were on full alert. In Falconi's hard silence, Gabriel heard a threat of danger.

Moments later, Simms was guiding the van toward the runway. Four men were walking away from one of three hangars. Gabriel took in the scene. At the east end of the runway sat their Lear jet, parked with lights off. North, there was a helipad with three grounded twin-turbine exec-type choppers. What looked like a large warehouse loomed beyond the hangars.

"It's jump-off time, Simms. Suggest you keep your eyes peeled. I got a bad feeling in my gut."

"You ain't alone, my man. Hundred-to-one says those dudes are packing. Another hundred-to-one says Lightning's boys have been forewarned."

Gabriel slid open the side door, ushered Falconi out of the van. As Simms doused the van's headlights, Gabriel and Falconi walked toward the four men.

With a sixth sense for danger, honed by years of living on the edge of life and death, Gabriel was picking up strong warning signals. Even at a distance of fifty feet he spotted the bulges beneath the jackets of the four men.

"If there's trouble in paradise, Falconi," Gabriel said

in a harsh whisper, "you'll be the first one checking into hell."

An ugly grin ghosted Falconi's lips. "Hey, don't sweat it, cowboy. Everything's on the level."

Gabriel returned the grin. "Right. I almost forgot. You're a legitimate businessman."

Cutting through the woods, sticking close to the road and toting his M-16, Zac Dillinger could see that everything was not on the level. Far from it.

Two shadows poured out of the woods, fifty feet ahead of Dillinger. Shadows with submachine guns.

Dillinger looked across the road, spotted the Dutchman as Boolewarke glided through the woods.

Boolewarke was already drawing down on one of those shadows with his crossbow.

It was war, and Dillinger wasn't taking any battlefront in this new arena lightly. Not here. Not anywhere.

Next to his two ex-wives, there was nothing Dillinger hated any more than big-time drug dealers. They were a scourge, and he'd seen more than one person burned out, or worse, dead from drug abuse. Sure, he had his own vices, Dillinger briefly reflected. He drank too much. He did too much womanizing. Maybe even sleeping past noon every day was a vice, too. But he didn't steal, lie, cheat, or murder for his vices. At least that was his rationalization. Drug dealers didn't seem to know any rationale, nor did they realize any boundaries.

Everybody and everything was fair game.

Maybe that maggot who calls himself the Devil is right in a way, Dillinger thought, creeping silently through the woods. Maybe the world is a whore. Maybe we're all whores, glued to our own little vices. Hell, a guy can just replace one vice with another. Replace gluttony with sex.

Replace sex with dope. Replace dope with . . . what? Thrill-killing?

It was all too crazy for him to figure out. No, life didn't really make a damn bit of sense to Zac Dillinger. Then again, he told himself, maybe it wasn't supposed to make any sense. Man was, after all, an animal, driven, even after millions of years of evolution, by primitive urges.

Hell, he thought, it would be nice to just hang around and eat and drink and screw good-looking broads all day long.

But he had a job to do. A deadly job.

Johnny Simms's life was in danger.

"Dutch," Dillinger hissed, "take 'em out with that bow."

There was no choice, Dillinger realized. Any way the problem was attacked, either by crossbow or assault rifle, V.G. would be caught out in the open. But if Simms and V.G. were taken hostage, they would all be faced with a standoff and the mission would come to a standstill. Or worse.

The door to the van was yanked open. As soon as the shadow hauled Simms from behind the wheel at gunpoint, Boolewarke loosed a broadhead arrow.

A strangled cry. The gunman toppled, slamming into the side of the van.

Quickly, Boolewarke cocked the bow, loaded another arrow.

The commotion alerted Gabriel.

And the welcoming committee spotted their fallen comrade with an arrow lodged between his shoulder blades.

Dillinger cursed.

Falconi's welcoming committee clawed for leather.

Chapter 6

In less time than it takes to blink an eye, Gabriel whipped out the .44 AutoMag and jammed the muzzle of the stainless steel hand cannon against the base of Falconi's skull and locked his arm around the druglord's throat.

Falconi cried out in pain and fear.

Four would-be gunmen froze as they dug inside jackets for iron.

"Don't! Don't!" Falconi pleaded with the four men, his voice a shrill whine that trailed off into the night. "This crazy fuck'll blow my head off!"

Gabriel said nothing. So Falconi had alerted his people at the airport. Gabriel had expected nothing less from the hoodlum. The two dead hitters beside the van were proof enough that Falconi was full of surprises. Gabriel could play hardball too. Using Falconi as a shield between himself and the foursome, he began backpedaling toward the runway.

Simms, Boolewarke, and Dillinger ran toward Gabriel. The ex-P.I. had hauled Gabriel's Ingram out of the van, and all three commandos were now loaded down with spare clips for the subguns.

"Is that jet fueled and ready to go?" Gabriel asked the foursome.

"What the hell's going on here, Mr. Falconi?" one of the foursome asked. "I don't understand—"

"Never mind. Just answer his fucking question!" Falconi gasped.

"Anybody ever tell you," Gabriel rasped into Falconi's ear, "that you've got a foul mouth? I bet your mother went through a lot of soap when you were a young punk."

"Fuck you," Falconi shot back.

"Yeah. It's fueled," the man told them. "Michaels, your pilot, is in the cockpit now."

"What about the parachutes?" Gabriel demanded.

"Five of them. Just like Mr. Falconi asked."

"This is crazy, Vic," Dillinger said, catching up to Gabriel, M-16 in hand. "These bastards will radio for help, you can bank on it."

"Left hands. Take out the heat. Real slow," Gabriel ordered the foursome, sidling up the runway. "Throw them on the runway."

The foursome did as they were told, unholstering and then tossing revolvers onto the runway.

Eagle Force kept their weapons trained on the foursome.

Dillinger cocked a grin, fished a fat cigar out of his jacket pocket, then flicked his Zippo. "We'll see you boys later. Can I pick anybody up something while we're out? Cup of coffee? Some coca leaves to chew on?"

Cold silence.

Dillinger shrugged. "Guess not. Uncultured slobs."

Mike Jameson wished to God he had never acquired a lust for cocaine money. In the beginning, some five years ago, it had all looked so easy, even though it had seemed so hard. With a family of five to feed and a mortgage to pay on a house in the Washington, DC, suburbs he really couldn't afford, money had been his single motivating factor to dip his hand into the cocaine jar—and not look back. It hadn't helped that he had kept a bookie and couldn't pick a winning horse if his life depended on it.

Despite his losing ways, he had always seen himself as a winner, a guy who could go after anything he wanted in life and get it. No matter what. But being tied to family obligations and job responsibilities could dull the edge in a winner, he knew, and had a way of dousing the fire in a man. There were people who depended on him, and his vices had to take a backseat to his responsibilities. Or so he had tried to convince himself. Unsuccessfully.

Torn between responsibility and the hunger for a life of style and easy living, like the big-time dealers he was supposed to bring to justice, he saw his bills pile up, his debts mount, and his bookie threatened daily to send a couple of gorillas to collect—in running blood and broken bones. Indeed, there was a price tag attached to a man's vices. But Mike Jameson was a tough guy, and he definitely didn't believe in quitting when the black clouds gathered over his head. There was a solution to every problem. Like stealing a kilo of uncut coke here and there after a bust. Like taking a little kickback now and again from the Colombians while on a trackdown of major dealers and their refineries outside of Medellín. And why not? Other DEA agents did it and got away with it. Why shouldn't he be able to enjoy a little of the good life, too?

But the good life, he had eventually discovered, came with a price tag. A heavy price tag. Or rather, in his case, the good life had dangled a noose before him.

It was in Medellín that Jameson had met Fernando Cortes Hernandez, son of one of the wealthier kingpins of the Medellín cartel.

Hernandez had a deal. It had been difficult, if not impossible, given the circumstances, for Jameson to have refused the "offer" the *capo di tutti capi* of the New Conquistador mafia had laid down. No way in hell would he have turned Hernandez down that day. Sitting in a dingy, stinking room in a barrio where few gringos walked out alive and whole. Surrounded by mean-faced men with huge, razor-sharp machetes, *asesinos*, he knew, who were trained at a school in the foothills of the Andes. Trained specifically to protect the cocaine-producing families. Trained, he knew, to oversee just such certain "offers."

Offer accepted, Jameson's road to hell had been paved that fateful day in Medellín.

Jameson had been put on the payroll of the New Conquistadors. Cooperate fully, without question, or face disgrace with the DEA, Hernandez had threatened. And criminal charges. Or worse. Jameson had a family to consider, after all.

So Johnny had signed his pact with the Devil.

Now he was looking back with regrets. With fear in his heart. Hating the past, he was also terrified of the future.

The present was something he dreaded, too.

He was a prisoner in the green hell of the Colombian jungle. If it wasn't for his master list of known DEA agents planted in South and Central America, Fernando Hernandez, he knew, would kill him without blinking an eye.

Jameson now stood on the threshold of extinction, his soul scarred by mistakes and ambition and now bared before the gates of hell.

Squinting, Jameson looked up at the lush green jungle canopy, shafts of sunlight knifing through the foliage in a kaleidoscope of broken color. For all its primitive beauty, though, there was death in the jungle, a smell of rot and decay that cloyed at Jameson's senses. For in the jungle the constant struggle between predator and prey was waged.

El Diablo, he thought, was the ultimate predator in the Colombian jungle.

Murder. Torture. Pain and more pain. The constant

threat of death. That was what El Diablo was all about. And El Diablo was a man who always got his way.

Cursing silently, Jameson felt despair edging into his heart. That one day in Medellín had cemented his destiny. Now, sweating in the blistering heat of the Colombian jungle, his fate was sealed.

Murder was in the air. Then again, he knew murder was a way of life in Colombia, almost like a ritual.

Colombia's second largest city, Medellín, had a murder rate of six every twenty-four hours. Fortress El Dorado was fast approaching that daily body count in Medellín. Hidden deep in the jungle, perhaps ten kilometers south of the Ariari River, El Diablo, Jameson had heard during the past few days, had turned his massive cocaine refinery into something other than a processing plant and fortress.

Rumor around camp had it that El Dorado was a death camp for the enemies of the Devil.

Two of El Diablo's soldiers, armed with AK-47 assault rifles, dressed in dark-green camous, and blending in with the surrounding wall of impenetrable jungle like ghosts, led Jameson away from his mosquito-netted tent. Jameson was certain El Diablo wanted concrete proof of that master list. Nobody's fool, Jameson didn't have the proof, at least not on him.

Ushered across the small clearing toward the canvas-covered bivouac, Jameson spotted the caravan as it returned from its trip to the river. Heavily armed New Conquistadors flanked the campesinos and Indians. Sweat soaked the serapes of the campesinos and blood streaked the dark skin on the backs of the Indians from where whips had bitten into exposed flesh. Because they were covered only by loincloths, blood had crusted black on the spindly legs of those Indians. There was good reason why those men were so emaciated. El Diablo kept his slave labor force sustained on the coca leaf.

A whip crackled through the air, lashed flesh. Jameson pretended not to hear the cry of pain. He had his own problems.

Sick with worry, he sniffed at the stench of animal dung, as thick as the clouds of *jejenes*, in the air. Then he spotted the oxen and horses as they trudged away from the trail. Both man and animal were burdened with the gold of El Dorado.

Burlap sacks bulged with the coca leaf.

Jameson squashed a *jejene* against his neck. The little bastards always drew blood. Jameson wondered if the *jejene* was a carrier of malaria. He hoped not. El Diablo didn't seem to believe in shots or vaccines. At least probably not for anyone other than himself and his soldiers. Then Jameson corrected that thought. A malaria epidemic was the last thing Hernandez would want at his refinery. Jameson figured Hernandez kept a healthy supply of quinine, Atabrine, and chloroquine on hand.

As if he knew Jameson was coming, Fernando Cortes Hernandez swept aside the mosquito netting and stepped away from his tent.

"*Buenos dias, hombre*," Hernandez greeted Jameson in a somber voice. The druglord was decked out in a white silk shirt and white slacks. "Unfortunately, it is anything but a good day. My apologies for not getting to you sooner. But a serious matter had come to my attention. A very *serious* matter has developed in *los Estados Unidos*, something we will both discuss shortly. And we do have much to discuss, do we not?"

Hernandez seemed angry. Jameson felt the sweat break down his neck, running like ice water over his shoulders. Jameson heard El Diablo's voice ringing in his ears, the words *serious matter* tumbling like dice through his mind. He was scared.

"First, there is this matter of a rumor going around camp that disturbs me."

Jameson hesitated, then asked, "What rumor?"

"The rumor concerns your master list. I am hoping you can put that rumor to rest."

Jameson felt fear touch every nerve end in his body like an electric shock.

A second later, Raul Pizarro stepped out of the HQ tent. Sweat glistened like an oily sheen on El Leon's beard and dripped in tiny balls from his long hair. His right hand, Jameson had noticed, never strayed far from the gold hilt of his machete. El Leon's left hand often touched his eyepatch, then one hooked finger would trace the scar that jagged down his cheek. If Pizarro caught a man staring at him while he touched his disfigured features, he would look that man dead in the eye and smile.

At the moment El Leon was fingering his scar. Jameson felt his heart skip a beat when Pizarro showed him a cold smile. The *segundo*, Jameson decided, was indeed the perfect demon left hand to El Diablo.

"Come with me, hombre," Hernandez ordered. Wheeling, Hernandez began leading Jameson up a trail that bisected the main path. Hernandez pulled a four-gram snuff vial out of his shirt pocket. Uncapping the vial, he spooned ground cocaine up each nostril, snorting the coke just right, laying it on his membranes and not drawing it hard up his nose so that it ran down his throat. The guy was a real pro when it came to snorting, but he had a real bad habit, Jameson thought. *Perhaps I can turn that habit against him somehow if the shit hits the fan.*

Suddenly the jungle seemed to come alive all around Jameson. Parrots screeched and other wild birds cawed from the darkest shadows of the jungle canopy like a hysterical symphony. Squirrel monkeys howled, dancing along the tangle of vines overhead. Mosquitos the size of small birds buzzed across the trail. Then there was the kokoa, the poisonous frog to worry about. The Indians smeared blowgun darts with the kokoa's venom, which caused paralysis, convulsions, and death within a matter of minutes. But it was the poisonous snakes Jameson feared the most. South America was home to some of the deadliest snakes in the world.

Pizarro fell in behind Jameson. As Jameson glanced back at Pizarro, El Leon asked in his deep, rumbling voice, "Something troubling you, hombre?"

"No," Jameson lied, and fought to keep the lump from lodging in his throat. "What would be the matter?"

"*Sí,*" Hernandez said, hitting the snuff vial again. "What would possibly be wrong? After all, you have the master list, do you not?"

"Listen, Hernandez, we had a deal," Jameson began, mustering the courage to keep a level voice. "I was supposed to leave the States for Europe after the hit. You had a plastic surgeon lined up in France who was supposed to help me out of this jam. This isn't exactly my idea of a vacation and a new start. Now what the hell's going on? Why am I being kept here like a common prisoner?"

Hernandez shook his head. "A common prisoner you are not. However, like some ignorant campesino who lives off the dirt of the earth, it would appear you have given this matter little thought, amigo. You have a family, remember?"

Jameson bit down his rising anger. He knew what Hernandez was driving at. "I had an explanation ready."

"*Sí,* a new identity given to you by the DEA. Relocation because of the South Florida affair. Perhaps your family would have bought that story, perhaps not. Whatever, you cannot leave until we have concluded business to my satisfaction. And my satisfaction always comes first. Now— the master list. Where is it?"

Jameson sucked in a deep breath. He expected the worst.

"It's not on me, Hernandez. Hey, it's real and I've got it," he hastily added, as the druglord froze in his tracks, rage burning in his eyes, "but it's in a safe place. Nobody knows about it but me. You'll get the master list once arrangements for my return to my family and my new face and relocation have been nailed down . . . to my satisfaction."

The druglord stared at Jameson for a stretched second. He hit the snuff vial again. "Games, games, always games with you people," Hernandez grumbled, sniffling. "Right now, amigo, I am faced with just such a game. A very deadly game. It would appear one of my main distributors has been hit. And I do not like it when one of my people gets hit. The next thing I know, I will have a full-scale war on my hands right here in Colombia."

"Hit? Where?"

"Never mind that now. This distributor is on his way to Colombia at this very moment. He was kidnapped by four mystery gunmen."

"DEA?"

Hernandez shook his head. "Your DEA does not operate with such straightforward violence and with such efficient military brutality."

Jameson knew that was intended as an insult. He was silent. There was no point in testing just how explosive El Diablo's rage could be.

"If they're not DEA, then who? CIA? Mercenaries? Who?"

"Do not panic, hombre, it is very unbecoming of such a brave *federale*. I do not know who they are," Hernandez growled. "I have to assume that, for whatever reasons, they are acting on their own. These *cabrones* have requested, through my distributor, to arrange a meet in Bogotá. The arrogance of such fools! If they are not killed in Bogotá,

69

they will be captured and brought here. I intend to find out who they are and to teach them a lesson. That is where you might prove useful, amigo."

"How's that?"

"Satisfaction, amigo, satisfaction. That is how. Follow me. I will show you satisfaction, my DEA friend. Satisfaction guaranteed, as they say in your country."

Jameson didn't like the sound of that. Something grim was waiting down the jungle trail. He could sense it, hear it in El Diablo's voice. He shivered as the sweat trickled down his spine.

They walked up the trail in silence for a full minute. Jameson peered off into the distance. Ahead, sunlight blazed into the mouth of the trail. Beyond that mouth loomed the stone steps and walls of an ancient aboriginal Indian temple. Against the harsh glare of sunlight, the massive stones seemed to shimmer in a white glow.

"You have heard of my readjustment program here, no?"

"I've heard."

"But you have not seen. Well . . . you are about to see, amigo. You are about to watch. And, hopefully, for your sake, you will learn."

As they moved past the mouth of the trail, began walking around the temple, Jameson felt that lump threatening to lodge in his throat once again. Stone idols, built and carved by a people long since dead and gone, stood like sentinels at the foot of the steps around the temple. Stone idols of the gods of death. Six-foot figures clutching gold maces and knives, teeth bared as if to devour anyone who would dare trespass into the temple. A serpent-eating eagle. Three bat gods, symbols of death. Jameson felt a chill run down his spine. He could almost envision the human sacrifices that took place here, the savages believing that they had to offer up the lives of their tribespeople in order to appease the wrath of the gods. It was superstition and foolishness. Or was it? Jameson wondered.

Human sacrifices were offered up every day at Fortress El Dorado. Only their lives were offered up to El Diablo. And just who was the savage, anyway?

"We have traveled many hard miles together, amigo, been down some dark and terrible roads," Hernandez began, leading Jameson away from the temple.

And into the bowels of hell, Jameson quickly discovered.

Beyond the temple the jungle had been cleared by hand. North, perched against the edge of the treeline, was a long block of stone cells. Behind the iron bars in each cell, Jameson saw shadowy faces peering out across the courtyard, eyes glaring, it seemed, in accusation and hatred. Armed guards stood at each end of the cell block. AK-47s were strapped around the shoulders of those guards. Machetes were sheathed by the sides of the guards, and like Pizarro, their hands stayed wrapped around the hilts of the machetes. As if they were eager to hack off the hands that gripped the iron bars of the cells.

But it wasn't the cell block that snared Jameson's horrified attention.

In the middle of the makeshift courtyard three naked men, bound and gagged, hung upside-down. There, suspended from a pulley, each man swayed gently over a large hole that had been dug into the jungle floor.

Hernandez gestured toward the naked men. *"Por favor."*

Slowly Hernandez led Jameson and Pizarro toward the three men. Deep cuts, running sores, and dark bruises covered those men from head to toe. A vile stench of feces suddenly pierced Jameson's nose as he approached the hanging men. Terror and pain stared back at Jameson. The fierce sunshine hammering down on his face and neck,

71

sweat beads popped out on Jameson's forehead. He flinched as a parrot screeched from somewhere in the jungle.

"As I was saying, amigo," Hernandez went on, his voice even, arms akimbo, a dark gaze fixed on the man hanging in front of him, "we have a long and, so far, good working relationship. My refinery here is huge and I am producing tons of cocaine weekly, more than I am capable of moving at the moment. I need new wholesale buyers, more distributors, bigger and better contacts in the States as well as in Europe. I have become larger than life, as they say.

"The men you have seen here are not slave laborers. They are primitive and often savage Indians, lured here by the belief that the coca leaf is a gift from the gods. They are campesinos sent to me from *cocaleros*, the cocaine farmers of the Andes. They will be gone from their families weeks, perhaps even months, at a time. They are paid, but they must work hard, very hard, to earn their pay. *Sí*, you have probably heard that I feed them only the coca leaf to keep them from becoming tired and hungry. This is a lie! Any malcontents, any loafers or troublemakers are brought here immediately and placed under armed guard for readjustment. Of course, like this hombre here," Hernandez said, and focused grim attention on the man hanging in the middle, "there are enemies to the poor people of Colombia. This man, this enemy of all Colombians, is a DEA agent, uncovered last week in Bogotá by a source of mine in that city. Perhaps," he said, smiling at Jameson, "you know this man?"

Jameson shook his head. He didn't know the agent.

"You were very helpful in freeing me from the clutches of your people in the United States," Hernandez continued, serious. "For that I am grateful. For that I will give you some more time to reflect upon your future with us.

But . . . I want the master list. I will not play games with you. Not now. Not ever!"

As Jameson looked at the DEA man, he suddenly found it strange that he had felt very little emotion for the dead agents he had set up to be slaughtered back in South Florida. He had hacked, under the threat of death, Big John Stiles's corpse into bloody bits and pieces. He had nearly vomited each time he'd struck the dead body with that machete, the blood spattering his face, the guts spilling out all over the floor like pearly white serpents slithering from his worst nightmare. But he was in too deep now to ever look back. He was a renegade. He was a criminal, and a traitor too. Fear for his own life had allowed him to push the horror of what he'd done, the treachery he'd committed against his fellow and now dead agents, out of his mind, sweeping it away like a man would sweep dirt out of his home.

Hernandez snapped his fingers. "Raul!"

Pizarro stepped up, grabbed the handle of the pulley. Without hesitation, he pulled a pin that released the pulley. The man vanished into the pit. There was a dull splash, like a large rock hitting a puddle of molasses.

"*Por favor*, step closer, hombre," Hernandez told Jameson.

Moving to the edge of the pit, Jameson stared down. He nearly vomited as the stink burned into his brain. Ten feet below, Johnny saw the man submerged in thick black sludge. In hopeless desperation, the man wriggled violently against his bonds, slamming against the sides of the pit.

Hernandez stared at Jameson with ice in his eyes. "Waste, hombre. Human waste. *Mierda*. Shit. Piss. Vomit. If he was down there for his first offense, I would have him brought up. But he is a worker and he has been caught stealing coca paste more than once. I will not tolerate the presence of a thief around me." Again, Hernandez snapped his fingers.

This time, Pizarro yanked the pulley's pin on the DEA agent. Jameson glimpsed the look of pure hatred in the agent's eyes a split second before he disappeared into the pit. Terror rooted Jameson where he stood. There was no splash. Only the groan of wood as the man's weight tugged at the pulley.

"Look," Hernandez said. Then, as Jameson hesitated, he barked, "Look!"

Jameson looked. And saw his worst fear unfold before his eyes.

The bottom of the pit moved, a slithering mass of entwined serpents coiling over each other to strike at the DEA man's face and neck. Jameson felt his legs turn to rubber. Bile burned into his throat. He heard the muffled scream, echoing up at him, it seemed, from a thousand miles away.

"The bushmaster and the fer-de-lance," Hernandez said, with no more emotion than as if he were reciting something he'd memorized from a textbook. "Their bite can kill within a matter of seconds."

Sure enough, Jameson saw the rope pull taut. Then, like a pendulum, the dead man swayed back and forth, his head, face, and shoulders wrapped in multicolored reptilian skin than seemed to glisten in the sunlight. Wood creaked. Jameson heard one of the prisoners mutter an oath.

"And finally..."

Jameson found himself unable to look the next victim in the eye. Somehow, he felt responsible. The jungle spun in his sight. He wanted to vomit. He wanted to run, screaming, out of the jungle. Pizarro brushed past Jameson.

The last victim descended into the pit. A splash.

Jameson gagged.

El Diablo laughed. "Piranha."

Pizarro chuckled. He thumped Jameson on the back, and the renegade DEA agent almost stumbled into the piranha pit.

El Diablo's laughter rang in Jameson's ears.

Jameson wished he could turn back the hands of time. But that, he knew, was impossible. He was committed, he realized. To losing.

He had signed his pact with the Devil.

Chapter 7

Vic Gabriel enjoyed a condor's view of the Andes Mountains. It was a rare moment when he could take in the sights while on a mission. On the tail end of a six-hour flight from South Florida, the Lear jet was fast approaching Bogotá. They were deep into the country named after Christopher Columbus.

Eagle Force had arrived in the heart of El Diablo.

Amazed by the sight of mountains that seemed to shimmer a bright green where the sun broke through the dark mist and washed over the slopes of the Andes, the ex-Special Forces warrior stared through the cabin window. Descending for the designated drop zone from an altitude of fifteen thousand feet, the druglord's private jet was streaking for a plateau that stretched away from the foothills of the eastern Cordillera of the Andes. Jump-off time, Gabriel thought, as the Lear jet surged through mist that soaked the spurs of the mountain range. For a second the jet shuddered as it plunged into violent air currents. Far below, Gabriel saw the mist swirl, as the air currents ripped through the veil of fog, blasting up from the gorge-cut, green-walled behemoth.

Johnny Simms and Zac Dillinger were making last-minute inspections of their weapons.

Puffing on a cigar, Dillinger said, "This is crazy, V.G." The ex-P.I. flicked ashes on the carpeted floor of the fuselage. His brow was furrowed, and he looked worried. "Tell me, old man, how do we know we aren't being set up, huh? We're walking into this one with our pants down." He shook his head, solemn. "Crazy, I tellya, crazy."

"I thought you loved crazy, Bad One," Simms cracked.

"Not when I feel like we're leapfrogging out of one lion's den and into another, Johnny boy," Dillinger replied in his usual gruff tone. "This old wardog's legs only got so much spring in 'em. My ass could damn well stay planted in the next lion's den. These old warbones sprouting orchids that Colombia's famous for, with the condors picking the skin off my ass. Crazy's one thing. Insanity's another. And lemme tellya, there's a difference between the two in my book."

"More than likely we are being set up, Zac," Gabriel answered, turning away from the window. "By now, Hernandez and his cutthroats know somebody's coming after them; I'm sure he keeps some kind of radio network that stretches from South Florida through Panama. He's a big businessman, remember? All right, so we've let him know we're coming. That's the way I want it, that's the plan. This is one mission we can't play by the numbers. It has to be feel the thunder, ride the lightning. These druglords are isolated on their own little islands, and protected, as you've seen, by an army of killers. The only way to tackle them is head-on and storm their island. Fear and violence are the only things they understand. They're predators."

Dillinger grunted, rolling the cigar around in his mouth. "Well, don't mind me chipping in my two pesos, Vic. If I sounded a little bitter, I was probably just thinking about my ex-wives. The ungrateful sluts."

Gabriel felt the grin dance over his lips. Dillinger, he knew, would be the last soldier to gripe about the toughness or the insanity of a mission. They were pros, and pros worked with or against the odds, no matter how long those odds were. They were all just edgy with prebattle jitters. They were on foreign turf, walking right into the enemy's domain. And the Devil had all the cards stacked on his side.

Just then, Boolewarke, his Barnett Panzer crossbow slung around his shoulder, ushered Falconi out of the cockpit. The Dutchman shoved the cocaine kingpin toward a seat. Scowling, Falconi flopped down into the seat.

"It took a little convincing, Victor," Dutch said, "but our boy here stopped gibbering in Spanish when I asked him if he'd ever done any *free-falling* from ten thousand feet. Our boy's a regular comedian, too. He asked if free-falling was anything like freebasing. I told him it's better. It's a higher high, but you come down a little harder. Like I really know what the bloody hell freebasing is, anyway," he added in a sarcastic voice.

"It's set, then?" Simms asked the Dutchman.

"It's set," Boolewarke answered, taking a seat beside the druglord. "The meet is supposed to go down tonight in some barrio at oh-six-hundred. A place called La Otra Economica."

Gabriel raised an eyebrow. "The Other Economy? What the hell is that?"

"A whorehouse," Johnny Lightning replied.

Dillinger chuckled, blew smoke. "A whorehouse. I love it." Suddenly the ex-P.I. looked deep in thought. "Don't know why exactly I remember this now, but in between marriages I had a sweet little thing from Peru, or Bolivia, or some damn coke factory down here. She talked about Bogotá a lot. *Si usted quiere Bogotá puede.* Meant, if you've got an itch, Bogotá will scratch it. Turned out she was a mule for some dealer in Boca Raton. They got to her before she could do her ten years," the ex-P.I. added, a rueful look in his eyes. "Christ, she could roll, though. Sweet-looking. Talk about scratching an itch." Dillinger whistled softly. "Big jugs. Tight, round little . . ."

"All right, Bad One," Simms cut in. "We got the picture. Just don't let Bogotá scratch some death-wish itch you may have."

"I get an itch, Johnny boy, it won't get scratched in The Other Economy, I can tellya that much. Hell, I bet even the cockroaches carry a shiv in this place."

The Dutchman slipped the crossbow off his shoulder, rested it between his legs. "What do we do about the flyboy, Victor?"

"Nothing, Dutch, he's on his own," Gabriel said. "As far as I'm concerned, his job's done. If he wants to get on that radio and alert the troops, so be it. I don't think he'll exactly volunteer to come back and exfiltrate us when the job's done."

"How about getting into Bogotá?" Dillinger wanted to know. "With all the firepower we're carrying, we'll look like a bunch of *pistoleros* coming to throw the town into a big revolution. And lookin' like Uncle Sam's ugliest gunsels, to top it off."

"We'll steal some ponchos and maybe we'll find an oxcart or some beaten-up wreck on the hike into town," Gabriel told Eagle Force.

"Oxcart?" Simms said, cocking a grin. "You were right, Mr. Vic. There ain't no numbers on this one. Next thing you know we'll be riding into Bogotá on a burro. The four *pistoleros* with no name. Shit, it *is* crazy."

"Loco it is," Gabriel somberly said. "And you can bet it won't get any more sane than this. Okay. Let's get those parachutes on. It's jump-off time. The cocaine badlands are calling us."

Boolewarke slapped Falconi on the back of his head. "Come on, Lightning boy. It's free-falling time."

79

Falconi cursed the ex-Recce commando.

"Why is it every time I look at you, I feel like tearing you up, chum?" Boolewarke growled at Falconi. "My hand just twitches to backhand your face every time I get near you."

"Because you're green with envy, that's why," the druglord answered. "You want what I've got. Women. Money. Fancy cars. Yacht. An endless supply of cocaine right at my fingertips. But you don't have the brains or the guts or the savvy to get any of it. So look at what you are. You're just a two-bit mercenary who knows he's fighting a losing battle. So you focus your frustrations and bitterness on guys like me."

Boolewarke looked away from Falconi. Shaking his head, he showed Gabriel a strange smile, one that seemed almost touched with sadness. "Can you believe this swine? Not only is he a comedian, he thinks he's Sigmund Freud, too. How can you beat twisted thinking like that?"

Gabriel slipped his arms through the straps of his parachute. "I know I'm sure jealous of him," he cracked. "When he's on his back somewhere with a bullet in his face and lookin' up at the Devil's ass . . . yeah, I'll be real envious."

The bright green grass rushed up at Gabriel in a blur.

Chin on chest, back rounded and hands gripping the risers, Gabriel touched down on the DZ. Knees bent to absorb the shock, he rolled. Standing, he shucked off the pack as the chute billowed, a mushroom head behind him. Ingram M10 in hand, he searched the plateau for Falconi. Scouring the plateau in all directions, he spotted Falconi.

And the Falcon was in flight.

First one to jump through the emergency door in the aft of the Lear jet, the Falcon had already landed on the DZ. And Johnny Lightning was running at breakneck speed up the foothills of the Andes. Gabriel cursed. The last thing he needed was to be tracking Falconi up and down the slopes of the Andes. He'd made a mistake to let the Falcon fly first.

Seconds later, Simms swept past Gabriel's position, the black ex-merc skimming the grass with combat boots, then hitting the plateau and rolling. With a strong wind gusting across the foothills, blowing in from the west, Dillinger shot overhead Simms, a good fifty meters away from Gabriel. They had jumped from about one thousand feet up. Not a standard five-hundred-foot combat drop, no, but now Gabriel found himself about to become locked in a personal little skirmish with Falconi. Damn it! *You live and learn,* he thought. *And sometimes learning the hard way is the best and only way.*

Simms spotted Falconi spreading his wings, too. Unslinging his Ingram, the black ex-merc drew down on the fleeing druglord.

"Johnny! Hold your fire!" Gabriel yelled.

"How 'bout cutting his legs out from under him?" Dillinger suggested. "Slow the punk down a bit? I don't think I'm in the kind of shape I used to be. I had the good life before I ran into you again, remember? Booze, titty bars, rock and roll, and IRS trouble."

Gabriel didn't think Dillinger was serious about cutting Falconi down with a quick burst, but then again, the ex-Special Forces warrior knew Bad Zac could get gung-ho in an eyeblink.

"Bad plan, Bad Zac. I need him whole and walking. I'll run the scumsucker down mygoddamnself, if I have to," Gabriel growled.

Just then, like some phantom falling from the sky, Boolewarke parted the mist. Sunlight knifed through a break in the clouds, illuminating the Dutchman for a moment in brilliant orange streaks. Spotting the Dutchman as he surged out of the glaring sunlight, Gabriel saw Boolewarke change direction, leaning on the risers.

The Dutchman angled his descent along the foothills, plunging in a straight line toward Falconi.

Dutch was going for a pickup, Gabriel thought. A clean sweep.

Vic Gabriel watched and waited for the drama to unfold.

A howling wind driving at his back, Boolewarke planed right, pulling hard on the right-hand risers. Streaming through the raw mountain air, he almost wanted to laugh out loud. The Falcon was in his sights.

And the Dutchman was swooping hard for the snatch-up. At the moment, Boolewarke saw himself as the bird of prey.

Falconi was making his way up a narrow trail, fighting to gain altitude and put distance between himself and the plateau. The ex-Recce commando had plans for the Falcon. He wanted to put the fear of God into that guy's heart and teach him a lesson. Boolewarke had listened to the drug-dealing scum run his mouth since they'd bagged him in Florida. He was sick and tired of Lightning boy's arrogance and smugness. And, of course, Dutch knew the scum wouldn't hesitate to kill him if he got the chance. That thought didn't do much to soften Boolewarke's hardheartedness toward Falconi. And that bit about them being jealous of Falconi? Not in a million years, Boolewarke knew. He wouldn't want what Falconi had if it was given to him on a silver platter. It was the guys who appeared to have it all who really had nothing. They were men without heart, without soul. Without the balls to stand up and do what was right. It was always easiest to do what was wrong. The *wrongness*, though, always caught up to a man. Always. Caught him when he was napping, Boolewarke thought, and least expected it. Like a thief in the night, the wrongness, and a man's life would be stolen from him.

Boolewarke tugged on the risers, planed left just a fraction. He was in line and on target.

At the last possible second, Falconi looked up, as if sensing he was about to be attacked.

As if the sky were falling on the Falcon.

The sky fell.

Boolewarke opened his legs. Like scissors, the Dutchman's legs snapped together as Falconi's face slammed into the harness around Boolewarke's crotch. Falconi squirmed, cried out in fear. Desperately he clawed at Boolewarke's legs.

"Hang on, Lightning boy! You dig into my balls, I'll drop you like a bad habit!" Dutch hollered. Then, planing right, he soared away from the trail. Falconi's added weight sent the two of them plummeting hard toward the plain.

Twisting his head, Falconi spotted a boulder, rising, it seemed, right out of the earth. And pointed right at his ass.

Falconi lifted his legs, but the boulder scraped his buttocks and thighs, tearing away cloth and flesh like a scythe. Viciously, Falconi cursed Boolewarke.

"Hope you enjoyed the ride, Lightning boy! It's free-falling time, chum!"

Falling rapidly toward the plateau, Boolewarke released Falconi. Falconi screamed, but it was only a ten-foot drop. He hit the ground on his feet, crumpled, and rolled.

Gabriel, Simms, and Dillinger ran up to Boolewarke as the Dutchman came out of his roll and slipped out of his chute.

Falconi was still cursing as he stood. He checked the rip in his slacks, showed Eagle Force bloodstained hands.

"You sonofabitch!" the Falcon raged. "You could've crippled me! You could've killed me!"

"I could've, you swine," Boolewarke returned in a flat voice, a thin smile slitting his lips. "And I probably should've. But I'm green with envy, remember? Now," the Dutchman said, turning his attention toward his fellow commandos, "what's this about a whorehouse?"

Dillinger cocked a grin at the Dutchman. "Remind me to take you out for a night on the town in Paris sometime, old man."

"Fat chance."

Chapter 8

It was after dusk when Eagle Force entered the heart of Bogotá. Checking the illuminated dial of his Rolex, Vic Gabriel saw that they were one hour and twenty minutes late for their rendezvous with El Diablo's cutthroats at La Otra Economica.

0600 had come and gone with a mighty peal of thunder.

Two hours ago, the sun had been swallowed up by an onslaught of black clouds, and twilight never emerged from the dark caldron of thunderheads boiling over the Andes. Less than an hour ago, those clouds had split open in a cannonade of thunder. Thick sheets of rain now crashed down on the streets of the capital city, pounding off the countless rows of red-tiled roofs, slanting into towering white skyscrapers that seemed to knife straight up into the underbelly of clouds. Jagged fingers of lightning crackled, strobed across the grim sky every few moments.

At more than a mile and a half above sea level, Bogotá is nestled in a shallow dish of the Andes Mountains, ringed by a green wall of rock. The thin air was the first thing Gabriel had noticed. His lungs were working overtime to pull in a steady supply of oxygen. He felt a headache coming on and realized he might be in for a nasty little fight just to combat acute sickness because of the thin air. The other commandos had already mentioned they felt a little queasy themselves. But it was suck-it-up time, and Gabriel knew that a dose of *soroche*, which was what the Colombias called "acute mountain sickness," wouldn't slow his juggernaut down any when they rolled up against the New Conquistadors. The threat of violent death had a way of clearing a soldier's head with a burst of adrenaline.

The stink of car fumes had marked the second assault on the ex-Special Forces warrior's senses. Even though a torrential downpour hammered the city, which appeared to Gabriel to be a mix of old-world Spanish colonial and modern industrialized twentieth century, the thunderstorm didn't seem to slow down any activity on the streets. Mangy mongrels roamed alleyways, and *colectivo* taxis and beaten-up Chevys and Plymouths jammed the narrow streets. Black car exhaust slashed away by the driving rain, drivers cursed and shook their fists, horns blaring, as they jockeyed through the congestion of flesh and metal to be on their way. And *bogatanos*, perhaps looking to score some of the highest-grade coke to be found anywhere in the world, lounged, dark shadows, in the crooks and crevices of grimy-looking duplex apartment buildings. It was no place for a lone gringo, Gabriel decided. The crime rate in Colombia, he recalled from his reading of the DEA report, had soared as quickly as the modernization of the city since Pope Paul VI's visit to South America in 1968. But the four of them were well armed. And before the night was over, gut feeling warned Gabriel, their firepower would be adding noise to the thunder that was almost constantly pealing over the capital city of the cocaine badlands.

Johnny Simms sat behind the wheel of the old Buick four-door. Like the other commandos, Simms wore a brown ruana. Vic Gabriel had bought the woolen ponchos and the Buick off a coffee farmer in the Andean foothills for five hundred dollars American. When the time came to enter the whorehouse, the ruanas would conceal their weapons. Of course, any extended look would spot the bulge of the Ingram subguns, which would hang from their necks by a thin cord when they entered La Otra Economica. The only thing Gabriel was looking to extend was a little bit of luck. Once they confronted whatever force was sent to greet them at the whorehouse, they were on their own. And no, Vic Gabriel didn't expect the welcoming committee to greet them with open arms and the smile of Jesus on their lips. It was going to be a down-and-dirty, head-knocking encounter of the worst kind. The death kind.

"Five hundred bucks Yankee cash goes a long way down here," Zac Dillinger gruffed, chomping down on his Cuban cigar and staring out the window as the Buick rolled off a main avenue and began heading down a dark street. Here there were no street signs, Gabriel noticed. Just broken streetlights. Red-brick shops and stone-slab dwellings. Garbage littering the gutters. Ruts and potholes that sloshed black sludge over the Buick as the car jounced along at a snail's pace. Traffic thinned out considerably, and a block later it seemed to virtually disappear altogether before Gabriel's thorough recon of the area. A rough-looking barrio, with its dark, dilapidated-looking, low-lying buildings; this was no man's land. No, Gabriel thought, this wasn't the ultramodern office and apartment district, with its view of the towering Guadalupe and Monserrate mountain crests that they had seen on their drive into Bogotá from the freeway. This was where life burned on in loud and violent desperation. And where life burned out just as fast on poverty and crime and cocaine.

"You might've bought the whole coffee farm off that old boy, Vic," Dillinger went on, gaze narrowed as he searched the deep shadows blanketing the streets for any sign of life. "For another Ben Franklin or two, hell, I could've been kept in three cups of black every morning for nothin' for the rest of my life. Now, I'm not a guy lookin' for a free lunch—"

"Sure you aren't, Bad One," Simms cracked. "Not Mister Drinks-are-on-me-but-give-that-sucker-over-there-the-bill. How 'bout that time in Miami—"

"Get a lid on it, Johnny boy. Whatever story you're dreamin' up now, I'm sure I've forgotten."

Simms chuckled. "I'm sure."

Henry van Boolewarke, sitting beside Ramon Falconi, who was pinned in the backseat between the Afrikaaner and the ex-P.I., waved some of the cigar smoke away from his face. "You have to smoke those bloody Communist cigars, mate? Christ's eyes, I'm having a hard enough time breathing this mountain air as it is without sucking that stink into my nose. Out the window with that bloody commie cigar, or I might just puke in your lap."

"Relax, old man," Dillinger said, puffing leisurely on his stogie. "I don't care if Castro is a fucking Communist and an egg-suckin' gangster. The best stogies in the whole world come out of Havana. Besides, these help keep my trigger finger calm. And you're not the only one who could be wheezing and suckin' the air here soon, too, y'know. I don't think us gringos were cut out for the lack of air here in the Andes."

"Nor are you cut out for a confrontation with the bazooka-smokers, if you're not careful," Falconi said. "I don't care how well armed you are. Or how big you think your balls are."

Gabriel cocked his head sideways. "What was that, Falconi?"

"The bazooka-smokers, they call them," Falconi answered. "Down here, they take the coca paste and saturate cigarettes with it. They say it's one beautiful incredible high, much better than the freebasing in the States, much more powerful and addicting than crack—which is what you get when you cook coke. I understand the bazooka-smoking also makes you crazy after a while—homicidal crazy. That's one reason why there are so many murders in Colombia. I'm sure El Diablo's men like to do some bazooka-smoking themselves.

"As for American money, most of these people are poor, but they get the best coke anywhere," he added in a voice that sounded touched with envy. "A gram of cocaine in the States is a hundred dollars. Down here, a gram is ten dollars. And you're talking high grade here, at least ninety percent pure."

"Who the fuck cares?" Dillinger growled.

"I care, cowboy," Falconi shot back. "Money talks and bullshit walks. For another hundred bucks, I could've been riding around town in a Cadillac, instead of chugging along in this piece of shit choking on the fumes of that fuckin' cigar."

"Listen to this guy!" Simms said, incredulous. "The cocaine warlords keep these people dirt poor and living like something less than a dog, and all he can think about is Victor shelling out more of our hard-earned cash so he can ride the streets in flash. He must be worried about his Colombian buddies seeing him with riffraff like us." The black ex-merc chuckled.

"Yeah, Falconi, you're a regular sweetheart, and you're just bursting with compassion for your fellow man," Dillinger said, and blew a ring of smoke in the Falcon's face. "If it had been me giving you that lift off the trail, I would've made damn sure I scraped your balls off on that rock. I think that would've made my trip down here worthwhile."

"Big, tough man," Falconi scoffed. "Well, cowboys,

don't look now, but The Other Economy is right in front of you. I'll see just how tough you are in a few minutes."

Sure enough, Vic Gabriel spotted the wooden sign hanging from the front of a building, a half-block down. La Otra Economica.

The street was deserted.

"I don't like it, Vic," Simms said, pulling the Buick over to the curb. "I smell set-up in the air. And I think I just saw somebody pull a shade back from the second floor of our whorehouse."

"We're ninety minutes late, Johnny boy," Dillinger said. "I'm sure the boys in the band are cranked up and ready to go in The Other Economy. If they're doing this bazooka-smoking to kill some time, we might find ourselves walking into a wall of bullets as soon as we hit the door. But, if we're lucky, maybe we'll catch 'em in the sack with some lovely little señoritas."

"Give us ten minutes, Johnny, to get inside and set the mood," Gabriel told the black ex-merc. "Then make an appearance. We've taken the silencers off, so if you hear shooting—"

"Come running."

"Right. Okay, Falconi, let's move it."

Cocking the bolt on his Ingram M10, Gabriel opened the door, stepped out into the driving downpour. He felt the rain and the cold air slash his face like needles.

And there was ice in his belly.

Lightning crackled, washing fractured light over the dark facade of La Otra Economica for a moment.

Dillinger shoved Falconi behind Gabriel.

They were late for their rendezvous, all right, the Angel of Death thought, head lowered as he forged onward into the stinging rain.

Late for somebody's funeral.

Gabriel felt the hackles rise up on the back of his neck.

Bogotá, for damn sure, was about to scratch somebody's death-wish itch.

Lightning flashed, brightening Raul Pizarro's swarthy face for a split second. Grunting, he let the shade fall back over the window. The cabrones had arrived. Three strangers. And the one who called himself El Halcon. *Bueno*. It was time to take care of business. Perhaps it would be a killing business, he hoped. But he had his orders from Hernandez. The cabrones were to be taken alive, if possible. Fernando Hernandez had many questions for them to answer, and Pizarro was looking forward to the interrogation. Pizarro decided he would let the confrontation dictate whether or not he would kill them. It would be a decision, he knew, made in the heat of battle. The cabrones were armed.

Even though they wore ruanas, Pizarro could tell when a man was carrying a concealed weapon. It wasn't so much the bulge beneath the garb, but the way a man moved. Cautious but self-assured, wary but moving with the confidence of a predator. They hadn't come to Colombia to make any deal, and they had been indeed foolish, he thought, to try and lead Hernandez to believe that they were there to arrange a buy. Using Ramon Falconi as their mouthpiece was a fatal mistake in judgment. No wholesale buyer or distributor in the United States or Europe ever came to Colombia to meet face-to-face with any of the New Conquistadors. Particularly on such short notice. And especially on no notice.

No, the cabrones had come to Colombia to hunt. Manhunt. He knew a predator when he saw one. After all, he was known as El Leon in the cocaine badlands.

The whorehouse, cleared of business by his soldiers,

could well become a boneyard for the cabrones, Pizarro determined. Hernandez would just have to simmer in his own rage if the cabrones were killed and not captured. Pizarro intended to live to kill another day.

Right hand wrapped around the gold hilt of his machete, AK-47 slung around his shoulder, Pizarro turned away from the window. He nodded at Sanchez and Paco, looking right past the dark-haired, olive-skinned whore, who seemed pinned with fear beneath the soiled blankets on the bed where he had taken her, two hours ago. She hadn't complained about not being paid her usual five pesos when he was finished. Pizarro felt a smile threatening to tug at the corners of his lips. He had taken her while pressing the tip of his machete against her throat. He had a drawn a line of blood just beneath her chin with the edge of the machete's blade to let her know he meant serious business. But he was far from being finished with Carmelita. Her curses still rang in his head, and he was still feeling her hate-filled eyes boring into his scarred face. But Pizarro sensed her fear like a living thing in that room. It made him feel powerful when someone was afraid of him. It was the eyepatch and scar that usually stirred fear in the hearts of men and women, Pizarro knew. He had lost that left eye in a knife fight with rival coquitos, years ago. Even though he had killed those men, he often wished he could bring them back from the dead and kill them, again and again, for partially blinding him.

Sanchez and Paco slid blowguns out of their leather pouches. Silently, they slipped out of the room, moving out into the hallway to take up positions.

Unsheathing his machete, Pizarro yanked the whore by her hair from under the blankets. She cried out in pain and fear.

"*Silencio!* Stinking *puta!*"

Pizarro shoved her toward the doorway. He had plans for the whore. She was a tool.

And she would be an instrument of El Leon's terror. The Lion was on the prowl.

"If ever a man walked into a whorehouse with his pants down, this is it," Dillinger hissed through clenched teeth, scouring the shadows of the empty barroom. "The Other Economy's really hopping tonight, but I bet the party's upstairs, V.G., whattaya think?"

Thunder pealing over the whorehouse, Gabriel approached the foot of the steps. Behind the ex-Special Forces warrior, Dillinger and Boolewarke, flanking Falconi, moved across the barroom. La Otra Economica was deserted. Or so it appeared. Combat senses on full alert, Gabriel, the Ingram M10 poised to fire, slid away from the naked light bulb hung from the low ceiling. Angling away from the dim light, he melted into the shadows along the wall. Crouching beside the steps, he looked up, searching for any sign of movement. A soft orange glow lit the hallway beyond the top of the stairs. He saw a shadow flickering in the light above him.

Thunder cannoned outside.

Gabriel felt his finger tighten around the Ingram's trigger. They weren't alone. The New Conquistadors were waiting in ambush. Well aware that they were walking into a trap, Gabriel knew they had to play the long odds if they were going to get to El Diablo's cocaine refinery. There was no other way. They had pushed, and now the New Conquistadors were going to push back.

Dillinger hit a combat crouch beside the closed door next to the bar. At the opposite end of the bar was another closed door. Empty chairs and tables choked the small barroom. At first glance, Gabriel had decided that La Otra Economica could have been a saloon out of the old

American West. Now, stalking through the chilly air of the whorehouse, the storm crashing down, he thought of the place as a death nest.

The enemy numbers had cleared the whorehouse out. But he wasn't about to give El Diablo's cutthroats any high marks for making sure the locals were kept out of the line of fire. He was certain the enemy had their own selfish reasons for emptying out the whorehouse, whatever those reasons might be.

Boolewarke aimed his Ingram M10 up the stairs and ushered Falconi across the foot of the steps. Hand dug into the druglord's shoulder, the Dutchman hugged the wall across from Gabriel. Dutch looked at Gabriel, his eyes hard with determination. Gabriel nodded at Boolewarke. They were ready to move up the stairs and take the fight to the enemy.

Then Gabriel heard a woman scream, "Noooooo!"

Startled for a millisecond by the shrill sound of terror, Gabriel saw the shadow flickering violently above him. A dull thud, like the sound of a heavy knife striking a melon. A second later, Gabriel saw the severed head bounce down the steps. Boolewarke snarled a curse. The woman's unseeing eyes stared up at the Dutchman.

The enemy was baiting them.

The enemy stormed into Gabriel's sight.

Two gunmen unleashed AK-47s.

A stream of 7.62mm ComBloc lead chewed into the banister beside Gabriel.

Boolewarke hit the floor, rolling away from the foot of the steps. A line of slugs tattooed the wall, autofire stitching on in a tracking line for Ramon Falconi.

Chapter 9

As the lead hellstorm washed over the positions of Vic Gabriel and Henry van Boolewarke, Zac Dillinger triggered his compact Ingram subgun. A long chattering burst, and the ex-P.I. hosed down the two hardmen at the top of the steps with lightning return fire. The .45 ACP rounds, muzzling at 280 meters per second, chopped up the chests of those gunmen. They danced a jig of death through their own shower of blood and cloth, slammed into each other by the hammering force of sizzling lead. But the sight of those goons checking out didn't do much to bolster Dillinger's confidence. All of them had walked straight into a trap, and there was no telling where the enemy would show up next, with automatic weapons blazing.

Dillinger had also seen Falconi go down, but he didn't give a damn about the druglord. That guy had sold his soul long ago, and as far as Dillinger was concerned, it was payback time for Falconi. There could be no pity for that guy. He had lied, cheated, and murdered his way to the top of the cocaine dungheap. It was fitting in a way, Dillinger decided, because the Falcon's wings had been broken by the very hands that had set him in flight and en route for the high life in the fast lane of big-time drug dealing.

Violent death had ended the flight of the Falcon in a

hurricane of bullets. And V.G., Dillinger thought, had been right. Falconi was now red with envy.

Suddenly the door beside Dillinger was cracked open.

As Dillinger's murderous and unrelenting return fire sent the hardmen above Gabriel and Boolewarke tumbling down the steps, the ex-P.I. spotted the tubelike object poking through the crack in the door out of the corner of his eye. Blowgun. Dillinger had heard all those wild stories about the primitive Indians of South America who killed with curare-soaked darts. He'd even run across a few Communist guerrillas during his stint in Central America, Marxist killers who could pick a man off with a poisoned dart from fifty meters away. No, those stories weren't so wild. There was a lethal truth to those stories.

Without hesitation, Dillinger ripped loose with his Ingram. A barrage of .45 ACP lead churned the door up, punching gaping holes through the wood. A sharp cry, and Dillinger saw the blowgun fall from lifeless hands.

The former private eye was unaware of the ambush that closed down on him from the rear.

Behind him, a dark figure emerged at the far end of the bar. The figure lifted the blowgun to its lips.

Gabriel and Boolewarke bounded over the outstretched body of Falconi and charged up the steps. Three more blowgun-wielding shadows slid out into the barroom. A hollow ringing silence filled the void in the firefight.

Dillinger kicked the door open. Flanking the doorway, he swept the black interior with a quick burst from his subgun. Cardboard boxes thudded and glass shattered against the hail of lead. The ex-P.I. found only one victim in the small liquor storeroom.

Pivoting, sensing movement behind him, Dillinger spotted the enemy numbers surging into the barroom as they streamed through the door beside the liquor rack. lifted his Ingram to grind those bastards up into yesterday's hamburger. Then he felt more adrenaline burn through his blood. He was out of ammo.

Then he felt something needlelike spear into his neck, jab into his skin like the bite of a mosquito. Fear, then panic, gripped him. The enemy had taken him out with a blowgun. Fate, Dillinger thought, had finally yanked his ticket. He had always figured he'd been living on borrowed time. But he had never expected to die from a poisoned dart in a Bogotá whorehouse.

A tingling numb sensation, and Dillinger felt his limbs grow heavy. He fumbled to slap a fresh thirty-round magazine into his subgun. Finally, the clip locked in place, he fired a wild burst at the attackers. Liquor bottles and glasses exploded down the rack. Dillinger saw a gray fog emerge into his sight. His legs turned to jelly. He was going down, he knew. For good, he feared.

After all the killing he'd seen, after all the dirty, ugly firefights he'd survived with an almost brutal glee . . .

I'm being wasted by a fuckin' poisoned dart in Bogotá, he heard his mind scream. *What a way to go! Belly up in a lousy cathouse.*

Zac Dillinger heard his angry voice echo through his brain, then blackness dropped like a lead curtain over his sight.

Bursting into the whorehouse, rain and wind slicing through the doorway behind him, Johnny Simms saw his longtime friend go down. Glancing across the barroom at the Bad One, Simms didn't see any blood sprouting from Dillinger's chest or any other parts of his body. Then the black ex-merc saw the blowguns aimed at the backsides of Vic Gabriel and the big Boer.

Whipping his poncho over his shoulder, Simms cut loose with his Ingram. Three, then four, enemy numbers were driven into the front of the bar, slugs ripping into their backs and cracking through their spines as the Ingram stuttered in Simms's fists. But the ring of doom had sealed itself on the rear of his fellow commandos: Simms spotted two more blowgunners crouching in the doorway beside the bar. And Dillinger, the rear guard, had gone to confess his sins, Simms saw. The black commando silently cursed the enemy, Simms had been to hell and back the first mission with Gabriel, Boolewarke, and Dillinger, and he'd known the gruff, womanizing former private eye and the Special Forces soldier for what seemed like a lifetime. Anger, then hatred, fired Simms's determination to scythe down the enemy. This could damn well be their last stand, he realized. It hurt him with a bitter pain to see Dillinger pitch to the floor with a dart sticking out of his neck. They'd fought hard and partied hard together. They'd saved each other during a fight to the death with the enemy before. Countless times. Now it was all going to end. Here, in a whorehouse in Bogotá, while tracking down some of the world's richest, sleaziest, and deadliest criminals, there would be no salvation for Zac Dillinger.

Firing on the run, racing for the steps across the barroom, Simms mowed the blowgunners down.

A blowgunner, half of his skull shot away, crashed into the liquor rack.

Then Simms found himself seconds away from facing the enemy alone.

The Boer stumbled into the wall, halfway up the steps. Boolewarke grabbed at his neck, twisted, then toppled down the stairs.

Near the top of the steps, Gabriel began teetering like a Saturday night drunk.

"Noooooo! You fucking bastards!!!" Simms yelled, flinging himself against the wall and triggering four rounds m his subgun, firing over Gabriel as he searched, '-eyed, for any sign of the enemy above.

Then the Ingram abruptly went silent.

A shadow crawled from around the far corner of the bar. Blood pumping from his chest and stomach, the enemy lifted a blowgun to his lips.

He should've known better. Leaving his flanks partially exposed had cost them. It was a mistake, Gabriel feared, that he wouldn't live to regret.

Numbness settling into his limbs like drying cement, Gabriel pulled the dart out of his neck with a trembling hand. Boolewarke was down. Dillinger was down.

Falconi was definitely dead.

And Gabriel saw Simms crash into the wall at the foot of the steps.

Teeth gritted with savage but quickly evaporating determination, Gabriel raked the barroom with a long Ingram burst. The blowgunner who'd dropped Simms was slammed to the floor, bullets tearing into his shoulders and chest. Dark streaks of blood were smeared across the barfront.

Gabriel turned grim deathsights on the top of the steps. The bastards were up there, he knew. Waiting. Gloating.

Steeling himself with an iron will born from years of rugged discipline and honing lethal skills in countless battles, Gabriel, bracing himself against the banister, climbed the steps. If he was headed out into the Great Void, he thought, well, by God, he'd take as many New Conquistadors with him as he could.

It was that simple.

It was that fatal.

It was all going to end in a matter of seconds.

And El Diablo would be free to export his white poison. The Devil's death camp would live on.

Nausea boiled in Gabriel's stomach. Light fracturing

and spinning in his eyes in a maze of color, his head felt as if it had been chopped off by a machete, like the whore below him, and tossed on a carousel. But this was one ride he wasn't about to get off of.

The Ingram felt like a lead weight in his hands. Gabriel topped the steps. Through the wavering fog in his eyes, he made out the figures, halfway down the hall.

Six gunmen with AK-47s cocked the bolts on their Kalashnikovs.

A figure parted the wall of gunmen. A big bear of a man, Gabriel saw. An ugly face with an eyepatch grinning back at him. A figure with a huge machete in his hand. Big crimson drops trickling off the blade of that machete.

Gabriel raised his Ingram. He tried to will his finger to squeeze the trigger. No good.

The world turned black.

He saw the needle, an ugly obscenity, as big as a shovel. Tears of blood streamed down a face. A face that was cracked and bleeding. A face covered with sores and blisters. The face flickered over the needle, came into focus through a crimson haze.

Jim Gabriel cried out. *Go back . . . go back . . . it's not finished . . . it's not finished. . . .*

Vic Gabriel pried his eyelids open. The same big cutthroat with the eyepatch he'd seen back at the Bogotá whorehouse was standing over him. Still grinning, too. Gabriel wanted to wipe that smirk off the guy's face. With a long burst from a submachine gun, as he recalled how the bastard had brutally murdered that woman back at La Otra Economica.

Gabriel checked the gunboat. Standard cabin. Drums of fuel tied to the sides of the boat. Aft, he saw three long-haired New Conquistadors grouped around a .50-caliber machine gun. AK-47s were slung around their shoulders.

The throb and chug of diesel engines and the fierce heat revived Gabriel. His head pounded. His muscles ached. He sat up and felt the rope biting into his wrists. Portside, sitting across from him, Gabriel found Simms, Dillinger, and Boolewarke, their hands bound with rope behind their backs. At least, he thought, they were all alive.

"*Buenos dias, cabron,*" Pizarro greeted Gabriel, his hand fisted around the gold hilt of his machete. "Be thankful Fernando Cortes Hernandez is a man of mercy and compassion. Those darts could just have easily been tipped with curare instead of a powerful narcotic."

"Cortes? These guys take that New Conquistador shit pretty serious," Simms cracked.

"Yeah," Dillinger added, "next thing you know he'll be telling us they've found the gold of El Dorado here in the jungle."

"Funny you should mention that, cabron," Pizarro said. "El Dorado is precisely where you are going. From which there will be no escape for you. You cannot run. And you certainly cannot hide from us. Nothing but hundreds of square miles of jungle will be your home, and your grave. And Colombia has some of the deadliest jungle in the world."

"How long have we been out?" Gabriel asked his commandos, squinting up at a sky flaming a bright orange— the sun, he judged, burning down over the river from twelve o'clock high.

"Hours, I would guess," Boolewarke answered, his gaze narrowed to try to keep the sweat from burning into his eyes.

"We just came to a few minutes ago ourselves," Simms added.

"And Cap'n Blye here," Dillinger said, jerking a nod at Pizarro, "doesn't seem inclined to answer any questions."

Right then, Gabriel noticed there was another prisoner on the gunboat. Pizarro followed Gabriel's stare to the aft section.

"Cabrones," Pizarro began, turning and walking toward the dark-haired, dark-skinned man. "I would like you to get a taste of life here in the Colombian jungle. A good life for some," he said, then shrugged. "A bad life for our enemies. You will watch and listen. I hope you learn something, too. Here, there are no second chances. Here, there is only one ruler. That ruler is death. Sudden, swift, and violent."

Downriver a flock of spoonbills spread their large pink wings, flapping across the river, skimming the dark reddish water. Sunlight danced over the surface of the river like sparkling diamonds. Thick green trees, like huge clumps of broccoli, lined the riverbanks.

Pizarro nodded at one of the gunners.

Terror filled the prisoner's eyes. He pleaded with the man for a second in Spanish. Gabriel assumed the prisoner was asking the soldier to spare his life. The cutthroat didn't appear ready to oblige that plea for mercy.

"A coquito," Pizarro told Eagle Force, "who would rather enjoy our surplus than move the cocaine for us. He never pays on time. He has cost us money. His uncontrolled lust for the gift of the gods will now cost him."

The prisoner struggled. He was clubbed over the head with the butt of an AK-47. Then the New Conquistador cutthroat hauled the man to his feet and shoved him overboard. Bone-chilling screams lanced the air. Gabriel heard the man thrashing in the water.

Pizarro grinned at Gabriel. "The Ariari is infested with piranha. You see, near the Brazilian border our country is blessed, or cursed, depending on how you look at it—" He laughed, glancing toward the railing—"by many of the same creatures that make the Amazon such a dangerous place. You would be most foolish to attempt to escape from El Dorado. The jungle, cabrones, would swallow you up as if you never existed."

The screams trailed behind the gunboat.

"I wonder if this is what they mean by gunboat diplomacy?" a grim-faced Dillinger said, asking no one in particular.

"*Sí*," Raul Pizarro answered. Then the grin melted from his lips and his dark eyes burned down on Dillinger with menace. "And we are very easy to get along with. Very, very easy."

"I bet," Dillinger growled.

Chapter 10

The dark journey to Fortress El Dorado over, Gabriel's gut instinct warned him that their nightmare had only begun.

As they had been led around the ancient Indian temple, Gabriel could smell the stink of death and suffering in the air. Whatever El Diablo had planned for them, Gabriel knew it wouldn't be good. He had seen the pulleys over the three pits outside, the ropes taut as if they were holding weight. Dead weight. Fortress El Dorado was no paradise of gold and glory. The damn place had all the markings of a death camp. And Fernando Hernandez was no gilded man.

Already Gabriel was searching his mind for a plan of escape. But he had seen at least a dozen heavily armed cutthroats guarding the squat cellblock outside. He was sure that in the days ahead, the four of them would be beaten, tortured, and starved half to death—if they even lived that long.

If they were going to escape, they would have to do it soon. Within a matter of hours. Time was definitely not on their side.

And Gabriel didn't have the first clue as to where the cocaine refinery was located in the jungle. It had to be near the prison compound. But where? Pizarro was right about the Colombian jungle. On a map, the southern fork of Colombia looked like an overlapping region of the Amazon. Both areas were home to some of the deadliest snakes and predatory animals in the world. Then there were the primitive Indians, who had lived in the jungle long before the brutal arrival of the Spanish. With their blowguns, they could strike like specters, killing a man from the trees if they felt their land was being intruded upon.

As Pizarro sliced the ropes off the hands of each commando with his machete, a New Conquistador soldier shoved the men inside the cell.

There was another prisoner in that cell, Gabriel discovered. The man had been beaten, but he didn't look underfed to Gabriel. Five prisoners inside an area of roughly ten by fifteen feet would make for cramped living conditions. That was if any prisoner at Fortress El Dorado could be counted among the living, Gabriel decided.

"Who the hell are you?" Dillinger barked at the prisoner.

"A special hombre," Pizarro said with a sneer. "Treat this special hombre with respect and dignity." He paused. Then, with ice in his voice, he said, "Or I might just cut your hearts out and feed them to you."

"That doesn't answer my question, cyclops," Dillinger growled. "How come I can't get a straight answer out of you, One Eye, huh?"

Filling the doorway with his enormous bulk, Pizarro squared his shoulders, his jaw clenching, his knuckles turning stark white as he squeezed the hilt of his machete. Gabriel steeled himself, expected Pizarro to come charging into the cell, swinging his machete like some berserk Viking.

"I believe I will answer that question for you, cabron."

Pizarro stepped aside. And Gabriel found himself

face-to-face with the cocaine warlord of Colombia. El Diablo.

Gabriel was surprised by the druglord's slight stature. Hernandez was much smaller than Gabriel had expected from a man of such notoriety. But there was a fire in the druglord's eyes, a fire Gabriel had seen many times in the eyes of vicious enemies. A fire that warned Gabriel that this was a man who would kill without thinking twice about it.

It was the fire of insanity.

Grinning, Hernandez stood in the doorway, hands on his hips, his white suit spotless. Gabriel felt like ripping the guy's face off.

Boolewarke slouched against the wall, standing in the shafts of sunlight that cut between the iron-barred window. "So this is the bloody Devil, eh? Doesn't look like much," the Dutchman muttered to himself. "But the Falcon didn't look like much either."

Hernandez looked at Boolewarke, surprised, it seemed, by the Afrikaaner's thick accent. "You are not a *Norte-americano*?"

"Afraid not. South African."

Hernandez nodded. "A Boer. A racist, perhaps?" he added, a thin smile slitting his lips as he looked at Simms.

"A Dutchman of Boer descent," Boolewarke replied. "And I could make you eat that racist crap if you didn't have a hundred guns surrounding you. Racist," he scoffed. "You must've been watching too much American news when you were in Florida, chum."

Hernandez ignored the Dutchman's remark. "Then none of you are DEA, like Señor Jameson here?"

Gaze narrowing, Gabriel peered at Jameson. There was laughter in El Diablo's voice. The ex-Special Forces warrior had the feeling that the cocaine warlord was leading up to something revealing.

"DEA?" Gabriel said.

"*Sí*. He is the one responsible for my escape from Florida. Señor Jameson is the mastermind behind that most unfortunate slaughter. I am most grateful to him."

Now El Diablo laughed.

Eagle Force looked at Jameson, who was sitting on the dirt floor. Jameson's face was cut and bruised and his shirt was ripped and slashed, most likely from the lashings of a bullwhip. Jameson looked worse than beaten, though— he looked defeated. Gabriel felt the rage burn off the bodies of his commandos. Eagle Force had been thrown in among the ranks of a traitor.

Sweat trickling down his face, Jameson looked away from the eyes of accusation.

"Every man," Hernandez said, "has his price. All of us live for that price, cabrones. It is human nature. I am sure you have a price, too."

"Don't hold your breath, chum," Boolewarke said.

"I will not do that, hombre. But you might be holding your breath," Hernandez said, lowering his tone of voice, his eyes gleaming with laughter. "In one hour, cabrones, there will be an initiation. All new incoming prisoners or workers go through it. It is something of a ritual, which my men look forward to. It is my way of wishing you a long and pleasant stay here at Fortress El Dorado." Hernandez chuckled. "We have much to discuss. Later, after the initiation, you will talk, believe me. Or you will die. Slowly and in great pain. Until then . . . relax. Get to know your cellmate. You will be spending a lot of time together, I assure you."

Pizarro glowered at the commandos for a moment. Then he slammed the heavy wooden door shut. El Diablo's laughter seemed to echo through the cell as Pizarro slid the iron bar across the door.

Eagle Force waited until they knew the enemy was out of earshot.

"How we gonna break outta here?" Simms wanted to know.

Dillinger pinned Jameson with an icy stare. "Maybe we shouldn't even discuss the great escape, with our cellmate from sunny Florida present."

Jameson drew a deep breath, appeared to think hard about something for a long moment. His features were cut by bitter anger. "Listen, mister, I don't have to sit here and explain myself to you four, or to anybody else, for that matter. So save your judgments, all right?"

"Well, that's just great, chum," Boolewarke growled. "That hit in Florida cost the lives of almost thirty men. Thirty good men."

"Honest men, I might add," Dillinger said. "Most of them had wives and children left behind. As for saving judgments, you can stick them where the sun don't shine. And I'll tell you why. We're standing here, asshole-deep in a jungle that may become our graveyard, looking at a guy without balls. A guy who's just as bad—hell, worse than the assholes we came here to nail. A guy who would stick a knife in the back of men he's supposed to be fighting on the same side with. Judgment? Yeah, I'm judging you, goddamn right I am. Verdict in: you're less than zero."

Gabriel knew it was time for him to step in. Fighting among themselves would get them nowhere fast. Jameson was in that cell for a reason. And Gabriel intended to find out what that reason was.

"Ease up a second, Zac." Gabriel leveled a steely gaze on Jameson. "What are you saying, pal? That you're in the same boat as us?"

The bitterness stayed etched on Jameson's face. "Take a look at my face. That should tell you something."

Bracing his back against the stone wall, Simms slid

down to the dirt floor on his haunches. "Tells us nothin', man. Tells us we've just got another problem to worry about. And another price tag."

"You've got more problems than you might think," Jameson said. "You saw those three pits outside?"

"What about them?" Boolewarke asked.

"One's filled with shit and piss and puke, another has poisonous snakes, and another one is teeming with piranha. If you haven't gotten the picture yet, you will. In about one hour."

Boolewarke swore under his breath. "If ever a place needed to feel a cleansing fire . . ."

Dillinger spat on the floor. "Is a dunking in those pits part of the big finish, pal? Is that what you're saying?"

Jameson shrugged. "I don't know. But this place is a death camp, guy, plain and simple," he said. "They export tons of coke and import death. Hernandez and his cutthroats would've made the Nazis proud. You want to judge me, go ahead, I don't give a damn anymore. It doesn't mean a thing now, but I wasn't exactly in bed with Hernandez. You might say," he added with a bitter smile, "that I was raped."

"We don't need to hear any long woe-is-me tales, pal," Gabriel said. "You made your choice, and it was the wrong one. When we make our attempt to break out of here, whenever and however that is, we'll deal with you then."

"Just why did Hernandez throw you in here?" Dillinger asked.

"I was the mastermind with a master list."

"Master list?" Gabriel asked.

"Yeah, a master list. One with the names of dozens of DEA agents under deep cover here in South and Central America. I haven't given it to the bastard yet. I can't. The list is my bargaining chip, my only way out of here."

Dillinger cursed. "You mean to tell me you're going to hand more heads over to Hernandez to lop off? Just to save your own skin? And after what you've done? Unbelievable. Tell me, what was your price in the beginning? A cool million? More?"

Anger hardened Jameson's eyes. "Right now... it's my life."

"You're life isn't worth one 'rand to me," Boolewarke said. "Besides being a traitor, you're a fool, too. What do you think Hernandez will do to you once he's got his hands on that master list, eh?"

"And how do we know you're not in here as an ear for Hernandez?" Gabriel asked.

Jameson shook his head. "Forget it, mister. I won't even bother to try."

"You never have tried, chum," Boolewarke growled, sitting on the dirt floor, "so why start now?"

Jameson glared at the Dutchman. He said nothing.

There was nothing, Gabriel knew, that the guy could say. His actions had spoken loud enough.

An hour later Raul Pizarro opened the door to their cell. The one-eyed New Conquistador pointed his machete at Simms.

"You. *Negruzco cochino!* Come with me. Move it!"

Simms glowered at Pizarro, hesitated, then stood, a bone cracking in his knee. He drew a deep breath and headed toward Pizarro. Two New Conquistadors with AK-47s flanked the doorway.

"Turn around," Pizarro barked at Simms. "Hands behind your back."

"What are you going to do to him?" Gabriel asked.

"*Silencio!* You'll see," Pizarro said with a laugh.

Pizarro bound Simms's hands behind his back with rope. The one-eyed cutthroat looked at Gabriel for a

Death Camp Colombia

second. He showed the prisoners a lopsided grin, then slammed the cell door shut and slid the bar over the door.

"Showtime, I'm afraid," Dillinger said. "A ghoul's show."

Gabriel, Boolewarke, and Dillinger crowded around the window and stared through the bars.

"I wonder what they've got planned for Johnny boy?" Dillinger asked, anxious, fisting sweat out of his eyes. "Christ, it's hot in here."

"It's always hot . . . in hell," Boolewarke mumbled, his expression grim.

"If anything happens to him or to one of us," Gabriel told Jameson out of the corner of his mouth, "you'd better believe you'll be numero uno on our master list."

"It's called a shit list," Dillinger added.

Jameson just sat in brooding silence.

Moments later, Gabriel saw a crowd of twelve New Conquistadors gather near the three pits. Whatever they were about to watch happen to Simms, Gabriel knew that El Diablo would do the same to them. Or worse.

Yeah, it was going to be a ghoul show, all right, Gabriel knew.

Simms tried to blink the sweat out of his eyes. It was no good. The fierce sun beat down on his face with a furnacelike heat. His eyes burned from the sweat coursing in large beads down his forehead no matter what he did.

Discomfort was about to turn into pain, he suspected. Just as there was no escaping the hellish blaze of sunlight, there was nowhere for him to run from whatever Hernandez and his cutthroats had planned. They were all in trouble. Serious trouble. And Simms was worried.

"Cabron," Hernandez called from across the clearing. "It's been some time since my men have had some exer-

111

cise. Their feet and their hands have gotten restless for action. *Por favor*. You will indulge them."

Right, Simms thought. In a pig's ass, I will, Mr. White Suit.

Twelve soldiers surrounded Simms and led him away from the three pits. Simms noted the laughter in their eyes as they unslung their AK-47s and piled them on the ground. They talked in Spanish, their voices edged with contempt for the *Negruzco cochino*. A group of another six cutthroats was lounging around a small drum. Those men were taking turns dipping cigarettes into the drum. Bazooka-smokers, Simms thought, as they lit the cigarettes and began pulling on them like there was no tomorrow. Great. He was going to get busted up by a bunch of goons flipped out on coke. With his hands tied behind his back, he didn't stand much of a chance against twelve men, even though he was a fifth-degree black belt. Simms determined that he wouldn't just stand around and let them use him as a punching bag. He would make them earn their brutality.

And Simms began to fear there might be no tomorrow for him.

The blow came without warning.

The punch slammed into Simms's lower back. The wind driven from his lungs, Simms crumpled to his knees.

A boot cracked off the black commando's jaw.

Stars exploding in his eyes, Simms reeled to the ground. Through the ringing in his ears, he heard his attackers taunting him to get up and fight like a man.

Okay, motherfuckers, Simms thought, *you want this Negruzco cochino, you got him.*

Fired up by a murderous fury, Johnny Simms stood.

Chapter 11

Rage twisted Gabriel's guts. It was a sight that made him want to kill Hernandez and his cutthroats with his bare hands. The nightmare was taking shape right before his eyes.

"Bloody bastards!" Boolewarke snarled. "He doesn't stand a chance with his hands tied behind his back like that."

There was nothing any of them could do but watch. And wait for their turn.

Even though Simms put up a fierce fight, rising to his feet and knocking out two of the New Conquistadors right away with roundhouse kicks that cracked off their skulls and left them eating the dirt of the jungle floor, the sheer weight of numbers crushed in on him within minutes.

Fists and feet pummeled Simms about the face and head. It would be a miracle, Gabriel knew, if Simms walked away from that punishment with nothing more than a few broken bones. Still, Simms fought with a desperation born from the terror of being beaten to death. The black commando pistoned a sidekick into the guts of an attacker. Then Simms snapkicked the steel-tipped toe of a combat boot into the jaw of another New Conquistador.

Hernandez shouted encouragement to his men, then began screaming and cursing his New Conquistadors as they seemed to ease up on their attack. Relaxing on

Johnny Simms in combat, Gabriel knew, was a mistake. Simms was a fifth-degree blackbelt, a mercenary hardened by violence and sudden death, and he had survived more than his share of life-or-death struggles.

Simms shattered a guy's jaw with a side kick. The cutthroat dropped as if a hundred pounds of hardened cement had crashed down on him.

Then an attacker clubbed the butt of his AK-47 over Simms's head. Simms dropped to one knee, blood spilling from his mouth. In the frenzy of action, a wall of dust began to boil around the human wall tumbling down on Simms.

"C'mere, you," Dillinger rasped, and hauled Jameson to his feet, clenching a handful of the DEA man's shirtfront. "That's our friend out there getting the living shit kicked out of him. Take a look!" Dillinger released Jameson. Silently, the DEA man stared through the bars. "Nothing to say?"

Slowly, Jameson moved away from the window. "What do you want me to say? I'm sorry?"

"Don't get smart," Dillinger growled, "or I'll kick the shit out of you, right here and now."

Jameson looked as if he was on the verge of despair. Feeling his blood pressure pounding in his ears, Gabriel stared at the guy. The ex-Special Forces warrior was experiencing the same brand of murderous fury as Dillinger and Boolewarke. But it would do no good to beat Jameson to a pulp; it would merely allow the three of them to vent their own rage and frustration. At this point they couldn't afford to waste energy. Sooner or later—and Gabriel intended to see that it was sooner—they would have to focus their fury on Hernandez and his cutthroats. If he was going to die there in the Colombian jungle, then Gabriel would make an accounting of himself. Boolewarke and Dillinger, he knew, wouldn't go out with a whimper either.

Simms was setting an example of what Hernandez and his cutthroats could expect.

"What the hell is that they're smoking over there?" Dillinger asked.

"Must be those cigarettes laced with coca paste that the late Ramon Falconi was talking about," Gabriel answered, staring across the clearing at the group of men around the drum. Greedily those men puffed on their cigarettes, laughing and joking among themselves as feet and fists continued to thud into Simms. When a man became tired of beating the black commando, he would walk away from the ring of assailants and another attacker would take his place.

"Christ's eyes!" Boolewarke rasped. "If that so-called bazooka-smoking is as strong as that scum claimed, this could go on for hours. Days, maybe. And I dare say we're next."

"I'm about ready to volunteer somebody in this cell," Dillinger said, glancing over his shoulder at Jameson.

But Jameson appeared to be lost in his own world, staring at his feet. Before Gabriel's eyes, the traitor seemed to shrivel up inside of himself.

"I . . . I can't believe it . . ."

"What's that?" Gabriel growled at Jameson.

"I can't believe this is happening. Why? Why?"

"You tell me," Gabriel said. "I heard something about human nature. But to me it's greed, plain and simple."

The beating of Simms lasted for another full minute. Finally Simms dropped. A cloud of dust hung over the outstretched figure of the black commando. The attackers walked away and left him to lay in the dirt. Hernandez ordered two of his men to pick him up and take him back to his cell.

As the blood poured from Simms's mouth, he was dragged toward the cellblock.

The dust thinned over the clearing. Hernandez stood, hands on hips, grinning.

Dillinger was taken from the cell next.

Gabriel crouched over Simms. The black commando's face was puffy, bruised, and cut. One eye was almost swollen shut, and Simms was missing two front teeth.

"Johnny? Johnny?"

Stretched on his back, Simms stared up at Gabriel through glassy eyes.

"Turn your head to the side," Gabriel told him. "You'll choke on your blood if you don't."

A sharp groan, then Simms did as Gabriel ordered. "Mutha..."

"Don't talk now. Any bones feel like they're broken?"

"I dunno," Simms said, spitting blood out of his mouth. "Shit... feels like I been worked over by a fuckin' tire iron. I don't think nothin's busted, Vic... mutherfuck," he snarled. "When we bust out—"

"We will, Johnny boy, we will," Gabriel said with grim determination.

Moving toward the window and taking his raging spectator's watch next to Boolewarke, Gabriel watched as the New Conquistadors began to beat Dillinger to a pulp.

But the ex-P.I. took a toll on his attackers, picking up where Simms had left off. Before they hammered Dillinger into the ground, three more New Conquistadors were laid out cold.

When the beating was over, they brought Dillinger back to the cell and slung him on the floor. Pizarro stood in the doorway. The one-eyed cutthroat seemed annoyed that his men hadn't beaten the white-haired ex-P.I. unconscious.

Trembling in pain and rage, Dillinger stood, bracing himself against the wall. His nose had been mashed, a crimson pulp, into his face. There were livid black-and-purple bruises beneath both eyes, and his white hair was matted a dark red in spots, blood trickling down the sides of his face.

Boolewarke was hauled away from the cell.

Gabriel couldn't bear to watch another one of his men being beaten into raw meat.

For several minutes, as Hernandez cursed and shouted and the sound of fists and feet thudding into flesh and bone seemed to explode through the bars like an artillery barrage, the prisoners sat in hard silence.

Dillinger spat out a mouthful of blood. "We're outta here, Vic. I want these bastards in the worst way. I want to dish out some payback, some real heavy payback."

Gabriel nodded. "Agreed. Tonight. I don't care what it takes."

"Open your mouth," Dillinger growled at Jameson, "and I'll snap your neck like a dry twig."

Jameson seemed unable to look at the commandos.

"Cabron! Cabron! Come to the window! Let me see you!"

Hernandez. Gabriel looked through the bars.

They'd stopped beating Boolewarke. The Dutchman tried to crab away from the ring of attackers, then somebody laughed and kicked Boolewarke in the ass, driving him facefirst into the dirt.

"Your men are taking good punishment. You are tougher than I would have imagined for *Norteamericanos*. And, of course," he added, as one of his men kicked Boolewarke in the ribs, "one racist South African."

"Tell him I said thanks for the compliments," Simms rasped through his shattered mouth. "Tell him his boys should take another hit off the wacky tobacco to kill any pain we might've laid on 'em. I hope we at least killed a couple of the motherfuckers."

117

"I am trying to have my men not break any of your bones or accidentally kill one of you," Hernandez went on. He shrugged. "It is difficult; they get caught up in their work. I hope you understand."

El Diablo laughed.

When Boolewarke was thrown back into the cell, Vic Gabriel had his hands tied behind his back by Pizarro.

Pizarro turned Gabriel around. "We have been saving the best for last."

The door slammed shut on the prisoners.

Boolewarke, his face a lumpy crimson mask, snarled a curse. "If I had the strength," he told Jameson, groaning, "I'd smash your head through the wall."

Jameson shook his head in disbelief. "You act like you're alone in this. What the hell you think he meant by saving the best for last?"

"Not you, chum, that's for sure," Boolewarke growled.

"And, by the way," Dillinger added. "We *are* alone."

Tasting his own blood, his head pounding with an incredible pressure, Gabriel hit the dirt floor of the cell. They'd laid into him good, but he'd managed to drop four of the bastards with a flurry of kicks. If his hands had been free he could have killed them all with sheer savage fury.

Feeling the sweat burn like acid into the cuts around his eyes, Gabriel raised himself up on his elbows. Tonight, he thought. It had to be tonight. If this was a sample of things to come, Gabriel knew the end was in sight.

Behind Gabriel, Hernandez stepped into the doorway. He took two hits off his snuff vial. He held the vial out. "Would you like some?"

Dillinger hawked a bloody lunger at the druglord's feet.

"Stinking *hijo puta gringo!*" Pizarro snarled. He took

a step into the doorway, but Hernandez clamped a hand over the one-eyed cutthroat's shoulder.

"Pain is good, cabrones," the druglord told the commandos as Pizarro stepped back. "Get used to pain. Like fear, pain is a master, or it is something to master. Endurance of pain is the measure of a man's character."

"Shut the fuck up," Dillinger rasped.

El Diablo chuckled. "You men have heart. I like that. You will need your machismo for the days ahead. Tomorrow," he said, glancing at Pizarro, "I will let El Leon interrogate you four."

"The Lion?" Boolewarke scoffed. "Figures, somehow. I'll tell you, heroes you're not."

"Being a hero," Hernandez said, "is only a matter of a state of mind, and the state of a man's heart. Now. . . I must turn my attention to more serious business."

Hernandez looked pointedly at Jameson. Fear shadowed the DEA man's face.

"The master list, *federale*. I want to know where it is. Now."

"I guess you were right, pal," Dillinger told Jameson. "They *were* saving the worst for last."

Defiance suddenly hardened Jameson's eyes. Sitting, he looked up at Hernandez. "Forget it. Only if we deal, Hernandez."

Hernandez trembled with rage. "No deal. Take him," he snapped at Pizarro. "Defiance of my authority," he told the commandos, "is intolerable."

Pizarro hauled Jameson to his feet.

Chapter 12

He was a Judas, a traitor of the worst kind, and he knew he deserved death. If Mike Jameson could have hung himself from the nearest tree, he would have. There were no excuses for what he'd done.

Before he was even roped and hung over the snake pit, Jameson had determined his life was over. Even if Hernandez intended to uphold his end of the bargain, Jameson didn't want to go on living. No, he *couldn't* go on living with himself, knowing what he'd done to put himself in that position in the first place. Perhaps, by denying Hernandez access to the master list, he would atone for his sins. Perhaps—and he felt the self-hatred burn like a living fire in his chest—he should have denied Hernandez long ago. Now it was too late. Yesterday was dead, the present held the specter of death before his eyes, and the future would never arrive. Hernandez was nothing more than a sadist and a cold-blooded killer. The four commandos, whoever they really were and whatever their mission really was, had been right.

A DEA man who sold his soul to the Devil was less than zero. And Hernandez didn't intend to honor any commitment with anyone outside of his New Conquistador cartel.

As he stared down into the stygian gloom of the pit, Jameson felt his bladder threatening to erupt. The vipers seemed to slither faster, his sweat splatting on the serpents like large raindrops. Indeed, they seemed to sense that they were about to be fed.

It was all Jameson could do to keep from pissing on himself. What a sight that would make, he thought bitterly, as the bushmasters and the fer-de-lances coiled and moved in one slithering mass of reptilian flesh below him. Hernandez would get a real laugh over a yellow streak.

Sweat burned into Jameson's eyes. The whip crackled through the air, again and again. Like a razor, the whip slashed across Jameson's back, slicing open long bloody furrows in his skin. Jameson found himself despising the taste of his own blood as it flowed down his shoulders and spattered on his lips. He couldn't cave. *He couldn't give in.* Not now. There had to be redemption. There had to be forgiveness from someone, somewhere. If there was some Divine Force, some Supreme Being who watched over and judged the insanity of man . . . well, Mike Jameson knew he was moments away from finding out the truth. Maybe he hadn't tried hard enough to do the right thing. Maybe he had always given his own greed top priority. And maybe, just maybe, in death he might find some peace. He hoped.

"One last time, Jameson," he heard Hernandez snarl. "The master list. Where is it?"

Courage, Jameson thought. *Find your balls and wear them, for once.*

Jameson shut his eyes to the sight below him. A man, he knew, can often become obsessed with his own fears. Jameson had never been more terrified of anything in his life than snakes. Since childhood, he'd been both fascinated and repulsed by them. Snakes, he recalled, are cold-blooded, and most species live in the tropics. He had learned as a boy that snakes don't hear by sound in the air, but by sensing vibrations from the ground. It was believed by scientists that snakes never slept because of a transparent cap over their eyes. Why was he suddenly dwelling on his obsession? In some perverse way, he was almost looking forward to his death. His death would be terrible, but it would be quick. The bushmaster and the fer-de-lance were two of the most venomous snakes in the world. *Fer-de-lance* was French for lance head. It looked something like its relative, the rattlesnake. Fully grown, the fer-de-lance was eight feet in length or more. But the bushmaster grew as long as eleven feet. Pit vipers are also sensitive to heat.

Jameson felt as if he were on fire from terror.

Smelling the fear on himself, he searched his soul for whatever courage he might have left. "Hernandez," he said, and fought to keep the quiver out of his voice, "I'd rather die knowing where that master list is than give it to you."

Silence. Cold, heavy silence.

"You are a fool, Jameson. But I just might grant you that wish. One last time. Where is the master list?"

Jameson felt the lump stick in his throat. His heart pounded in his ears. He said nothing, just wished to get it over with.

Jameson cracked his eyelids open, saw the shadow grow beside him. It was Pizarro.

"Go ahead, asshole," he told Pizarro. "I hope to God you get yours."

Pizarro spat on Jameson. Then, smiling, he pulled the pin.

Jameson wanted to scream, but he feverishly wished to deny Hernandez the satisfaction of hearing a sound of pure terror echo up from the pit.

He shut his eyes. He fell, hoping he was trapped in a nightmare. Hoping he would awaken. Hoping . . .

Then his legs were jarred to the bone as the rope

pulled taut and jerked him to a stop. He felt the bile burst into his mouth, choking him and pouring like battery acid into his nose.

They struck his face and neck. Fangs sank into his flesh like hypodermic needles.

It was no bad dream.

He was being bitten, again and again, by his worst fear.

Mike Jameson screamed.

"He took it to the grave with him. I didn't think the guy had it inside," Dillinger said. "I didn't think he had the balls."

Nightfall had blanketed the jungle. Eagle Force sat in the darkness of their cell. Gabriel stared at the flickering kerosene light that burned beyond the cell door's window. Like his commandos, he was hurting bad. Beaten. Hungry. But not defeated. Not by a long shot.

Mosquitoes and flies buzzed through the cell, picking at the blood and dust caked on the faces and necks of the commandos. Beyond the prison, the jungle had boiled to life with its nocturnal denizens. Monkeys howled, birds screeched, and insects chattered in an eerie jumbled symphony of noise.

"It's called last-second atonement," Gabriel said. He ached from head to toe, and the blood on his face had crusted dry over countless cuts. Nothing was broken, though.

"When a guy's lived his whole life wrong," Gabriel went on, "I would imagine that facing death in that situation can make you think about what's waiting beyond— and dreading it. There is a price, for everything we do. Whoever said there are no atheists in a foxhole hit the nail on the head."

Simms groaned as he sat up. "We've gotta think about getting outta here or we may be more snake chow, Vic."

For hours, since the gruesome execution of Mike Jameson, Gabriel had done nothing but rack his brain for an escape plan.

"Speaking of chow," Dillinger said, and squashed a mosquito against his neck, "when do they serve dinner here at the Holiday Inn?"

"Whatever they'll give us, you can bet your ass it won't be surf-and-turf," Simms said.

"I'd settle for a big fat Cuban stogie right about now," Dillinger growled.

"Hernandez doesn't intend to let us live long enough to complain about the accommodations," Boolewarke said.

Their chances of some clever breakout were nonexistent, Gabriel knew. There was only one option open to them. And it was a long shot—with the suicide odds stacked against them.

"All right, listen up," Gabriel began. "The way I see it, there's only one chance. We bulled our way in here, we'll have to go out the same. Somehow, we'll have to lure a guard in here, jump him . . . and take his weapon."

Dillinger seemed to perk up. "Blast our way out. Hell, I'm afraid you're right, V.G. There's no other choice. We'll have to hit and run."

"What about the other prisoners?" Boolewarke wanted to know.

"We'll set them free, too."

"I thought there were DEA men and so-called high-ranking officials from Colombia here. Shit, we'll be leading a whole caravan into the jungle," Simms pointed out. "That's a lot of baggage to carry along, Vic."

"And I'm sure a good number of them are sick and starving or half-beaten to death," Boolewarke added. "Won't make for good fighting *kamaraden*."

"There's enough guns guarding this cellblock," Gabriel said. "If they want to fight, they can pick up whatever weapons we leave behind for them after we grind a few New Conquistador bones into the dirt. But we'll make it clear that we don't want any of them stumbling into our line of fire when it comes time to headhunt for Hernandez."

"What about the coke factory?" Dillinger asked.

Gabriel shrugged and felt the pain grind him to the bone. "We'll find it."

"And level it?" Simms asked.

"Damn right," Gabriel answered. "Burn the Devil's palace down right to the ground."

Suddenly they heard screaming and cursing, sounds of pure terror that chilled the air.

Eagle Force stood, moved toward the door.

A second later, Pizarro stood, leering through the bars, his scarred face illuminated grotesquely by the wavering kerosene light. He held up a large burlap sack for the prisoners to see.

One by one, the screams beyond their cell door faded, died.

"Now there are four less mouths to feed," Pizarro told Eagle Force. "The bushmaster is a most deadly snake. Be careful," he said. "These bars are just wide enough to allow a visitor for you. I suggest you might try sleeping with your eyes open?"

Pizarro grinned, chuckled, walked away from the door.

"Yeah, they're regular tooth fairies," Dillinger growled.

Just wide enough, Gabriel thought.

Gabriel turned away from the door. "Listen," the ex-Special Forces warrior said to his commandos. "One Eye just gave me an idea."

Chapter 13

Hernandez took a healthy blow off his snuff vial. Sweeping the mosquito netting aside, he stepped into his sprawling cocaine refinery. At least three times a day, sometimes four, he and El Leon inspected production. Around the clock, a dozen chemists labored to turn the coca base into pure cocaine. They worked in twelve-hour shifts of twenty-five men for one month solid. Then they were replaced for another month by a fresh crew of chemists. Peasant laborers were brought in by gunboat loads of a hundred or more. Good chemists were hard to find and they were, indeed, Hernandez thought, the gilded men. But the campesinos were worth nothing more to Hernandez than the sweat off their brow. Once they stopped sweating, Hernandez wouldn't think twice about throwing them to the snakes or the piranhas.

Beyond the high stone walls of the refinery, massive quantities of coca leaves, grown by peasant farmers in the highlands of the Andes and flown to Fortress El Dorado by transport planes, had been salted and laid out on cheesecloth nets to "sweat." The coca leaves were now ready for the next stage of the refining process.

Scouring the faces of his work force, Hernandez smiled to himself. It was quite an operation. Fortress El Dorado was pumping out at least two tons of cocaine a week. Cooking cocaine took patience, patience which Hernandez didn't have. *La salada*, the salting, was always the first step. Sprinkle the coca leaves with *potasa*, potash. The potash melted the alkaloids in the leaf. *La mojadura*, the soaking, was the second phase. Kerosene, poured on the leaves, held the potash in a sort of floating state, which drew the alkaloids out. *La prensa*, the pressing, came next. When the kerosene was pressed out of the leaves, it was siphoned off into drums. The fourth stage, *la quaraperia*, involved taking the alkaloids out of the kerosene and putting them in water and sulphuric acid. *La secaderia*, the drying, was the last step. Left alone for a day, the cocaine and other alkaloids would turn milky white, then would be left to sweat in the sun until it dried into something like moist clay. Near the end of the day, the coca base would be moved into the refinery greenhouse to be dried under sunlamps.

Turning the *pasta* into pure cocaine snow involved even more grim patience. That was why Hernandez kept the best chemists he could find under lock and key. He paid them well, perhaps too well, he sometimes thought. But he demanded that they produce. If they didn't live up to his expectations, then they knew what they could expect. Which was why he kept the refinery guarded, twenty-four hours a day, by twenty heavily armed sentries. The chemists were only as good as their last batch of pure cocaine, Hernandez had always believed.

At the moment, El Diablo's chemists were hard at work to turn the base into "snow." In one far corner of the refinery stretched the drums of acetone and highly flammable ether that was used in the process. In another corner, the end product was packaged in thick plastic bags. It had often occurred to Hernandez that his refinery could become an inferno within seconds through neglect or incompetence. Or sabotage. Or attack. Indeed, two of his chemists had at one time suffered horrible burns as a result of carelessness. Any carelessness here, and they would not live to be careless again, Hernandez knew.

"Common *mercenarios*?"

Hernandez stopped next at a long table where *la pasta de cocaina* was ready for the final phase.

"*Mercenarios, sí,*" he continued, speaking to El Leon. "Common, no. Send one of your men over there tonight. But only use one. I do not want the *mercenarios* killed. *Comprende?*"

Pizarro looked disappointed.

"At least not yet."

Hernandez thought back on the beating of the four *mercenarios*. One look at them, and he knew they were not *federales*. Tough hombres, they were. Hernandez had nine soldiers on his hands who would be laid out for days, even weeks as a result of the toughness those hombres had displayed.

It would be interesting, he thought, to keep the four of them dancing, wondering what would happen to them during the next few days. He had always believed in measuring his enemies. Look for their weak point. Search out and pinpoint their fears or obsessions or vices, and use those things against them. It was the only way to keep the edge over an adversary. When he was satisfied that they had come to Colombia alone, when he knew exactly who or what they were ... then El Leon could have his fun with them. But not until then. His operation had not even peaked. Within a matter of months, as the campesinos cleared away more of the jungle, two more refineries would be built of stone and covered over by thick canvas to protect them from the elements. Inside another year, he estimated he would be exporting in excess of thirty tons of cocaine a month. He couldn't even begin to calculate the billions he would reap in profits. Now that the Europeans were demanding more and higher grade cocaine, the whole world seemed to be practically his for the taking. Every man, Hernandez had always believed, needed a dream. Every great man needed to fulfill both dreams and his visions of conquest.

"Remember, Raul, only one."

Pizarro, he could tell, didn't like it.

But El Leon nodded, because the Lion understood that El Diablo was the hand that fed.

Swatting at the mosquito, Gabriel saw the shadow grow on the floor of the hallway beneath the kerosene light. It had been a long night, and Gabriel had been restless from fear and an itching wish for action.

He was just about to get the chance to scratch that itch.

Dawn had broken over the Colombian jungle, and a dirty gray light filtered through the barred window over his commandos. Alerted by the drum of boots over hard-packed dirt, Boolewarke, Dillinger, and Simms stirred from their slumber. This was it.

Breakout.

Riposte.

It was time to take two eyes for an eye.

They had worked their watch in three-hour shifts. There was only one way out of the death camp. And Gabriel knew his commandos were ready. Hate and vengeance can be the most powerful motivating forces a man can experience, Gabriel knew. He was motivated.

A face leered through the bars beside him.

"Cabrones," the guard said. He showed them the small burlap sack, then the grin melted off his lips as he discovered one of the prisoners appeared to be missing.

The guard didn't have but a split second to taste his panic.

In the blink of an eye, Gabriel's arm shot through the

bars. Like a boa constrictor, that arm wrapped itself around the back of the guard's neck. The sharp cry of fear and pain was strangled off in the guard's throat as Gabriel mashed his face into the bars. Blood sprayed over Gabriel's face, the guard's nose squelching like rotten fruit. Fear turned to terror in the guard's eyes as he dropped the sack and clawed at Gabriel's arm.

"The bushmaster! The bushmaster!" the sentry managed to cry.

"Open the door or I'll snap your neck!" Gabriel snarled.

Face pressed into the bars, his head twisted sideways and eyes looking toward the ground beside him, the guard slid the bar off the door. As the bar thudded to the dirt floor of the corridor, Gabriel released his stranglehold on the guard and gave the door a vicious shove.

The guard reeled to the ground. He screamed.

Eagle Force flooded out of the cell.

The bushmaster lunged, sank its fangs into the guard's leg.

Right on Gabriel's heels, Boolewarke crushed the bushmaster's head with a mighty stomp of his commando boot. There was another sickening crack of bone as Gabriel drilled the steel-tipped toe of his commando boot into the guard's temple, silencing his screams forever.

But Gabriel expected the reinforcements to show themselves any second. Adrenaline exploding through his veins, Gabriel stripped the AK-47 off the guard's shoulder and Dillinger slid the dead man's machete out of its sheath.

Gabriel searched the narrow corridor in both directions. Hearing voices calling out from both ends of the corridor, he broke into a dead run. With a sweeping motion of his hand, Gabriel began sliding the bars off the cell doors.

Then, at almost the same instant, the doors at both ends of the corridor were flung open.

Gabriel triggered his Kalashnikov as the shadow filled the doorway ahead of him. The gray light in the doorway burst into crimson. As slugs stitched a ragged red line across the chest of Gabriel's target, Dillinger whirled. Releasing the machete in a sideways whipping motion, the ex-P.I. sent the machete spinning. Downrange, the blade thunked into the chest of another New Conquistador. Hand twitching for the blade impaled through his heart, the cutthroat triggered a short burst toward the ceiling, blasting a kerosene lamp into jagged pieces of flying shrapnel that stung Dillinger's face like angry hornets.

Reaching his victim, Gabriel stripped the AK-47 off the corpse. Wheeling, he chucked the Kalashnikov at Boolewarke.

Simms and Dillinger, running side by side, violently sliding the bars off the cell doors, almost ran head-on into blazing twin fingers of death.

Suddenly, autofire threatened to mow Eagle Force down in a pincer of sizzling lead before they even broke out of the starting gate.

A face of animal rage burst into Gabriel's sight. And his field of fire. The New Conquistador managed to squeeze off a three-round burst, but he was already dead on his feet, Gabriel's AK-47 exploding that cutthroat's face into something that looked like raw hamburger, the enemy's slugs peppering the stone wall above the ex-Special Forces warrior's head. Flinching, stone chips slicing across his face like a vulture's talons, feeling the slipstream of lead against the side of his face like the icy touch of a corpse, Gabriel checked the action down the corridor out of the corner of his eye.

Having yanked the wooden doors wide, Dillinger and Simms were shielding themselves from the barrage of autofire. The doors covering the ex-P.I. and the black commando thudded under the relentless stammering leadstorm. Believing they had the prisoners pinned down and weaponless, the two guards charged into the corridor.

It was a suicide play.

Gabriel and Boolewarke chopped those two gunmen up into bloody dancing sieves. Instantly, Dillinger and Simms scooped up the discarded Russian assault rifles, a millisecond after the corpses crunched to the dirt floor.

Retreating toward Gabriel and Boolewarke, Dillinger and Simms covered the rear while sliding the bars off cell doors. Some of the prisoners in those cells, Gabriel knew, would never emerge alive. The prisoners that did slip out into the corridor appeared half-dead. They stood emaciated, human scarecrows, their faces gaunt, bruised, ghostly masks in the flickering kerosene light. Gabriel counted thirteen men who moved like wooden figures out of the cells. They stank of sweat, blood, and urine. Some were half-naked, and the scars from the razorlike bites of bullwhips stood out, livid streaks of dead flesh across their backs. But where fear and despair had etched itself into their punished faces during their months of imprisonment, hope now lit their eyes.

There wasn't even a second to give orders or explain to those prisoners what was happening or who their rescuers were, Gabriel discovered. Crouched, he peered around the doorway, the jungle a black forbidding wall that ringed the prison compound. Out of the gloom a shadow appeared. A pencil-tip orange flame stabbed through the murk. Slugs raked the stone above Gabriel's head. Unflinching, he cut the enemy down with a three-round burst, the 7.62mm ComBloc lead tunneling open bloodgouting holes in his chest.

Dillinger and Simms ran up behind Gabriel and Boolewarke.

"What about them?" Dillinger asked, jerking a nod at the prisoners flooding into the corridor.

"You people are on your own," Gabriel barked at the prisoners. "I suggest you get to the river. I saw two gunboats there. Take one, and get the hell out of here. It's our show from here on out."

"Forget the hero crap, mister. You're not the only one who has a bone to pick with Hernandez and his bastards."

Gabriel pinned the man who had spoken so defiantly with a steely gaze.

"McCoy. DEA," the man growled.

For a second, Gabriel scoured the agent's face, as he shoved his way through the other prisoners. The full beard, the hollow ring around the agent's eyes, and the scabs and fresh cuts on his face testified to his suffering at the hands of El Diablo.

"I'm the last DEA man alive here. I've seen nine of my own die in this fuckin' hellhole. I go with you, you got me? Besides, I know where the refinery is. I've been there and I've had the tour. I don't think you have."

"Where is it?" Gabriel demanded to know.

"Back down the trail, toward the river, maybe a half-klick the trail forks to the left. Real narrow. If you're not looking for it, you'll miss it. Go about another klick and it'll put you right there, right in the fucking Devil's lap. I'm not asking you, I'm telling you. I'm going."

Gabriel didn't have the time to argue. The guy was determined. And Gabriel could appreciate the man's loyalty to his fellow agents. McCoy had seen fellow warriors, perhaps even longtime friends, perish at the sadistic hand of Hernandez. He had earned the right to vengeance.

Then that right was snatched away from him.

Perhaps they had been driven near the edge of insanity after being high for so long on the bazooka-smoking. Perhaps they were motivated by their own fear of El

133

Diablo. Gabriel wasn't sure, but he was suddenly faced with being crushed beneath the floodtide of a savage horde of murder-crazed gunmen.

From the far end of the corridor at least a dozen New Conquistadors surged through the doorway. Autofire roared.

The prisoners behind Eagle Force began dropping like flies as a hail of ComBloc lead ripped into them.

Blood sprayed the stone walls.

Men screamed.

Prisoners, some twitching in death throes, slammed into the doors or were hammered to the floor.

Gabriel tasted the blood on his lips. Then he saw McCoy corkscrew to the floor.

Chapter 14

The Devil's horde parted the wall of flesh with merciless autofire. Through the stygian gloom, their faces masks of demonic fury, the New Conquistadors triggered their AK-47s on the run. A din of screams and weapons fire assaulted Gabriel's senses.

Churned up into spasming bloody meat, prisoners pitched into Eagle Force like a fresh wall of brick kicked down by a gale-force wind. Blood smeared Gabriel's face and stung his eyes.

But the dead and the dying provided a second of cover for Eagle Force to return fire. And the tide of slaughter washed back over the enemy.

Through the spinning bodies, Eagle Force directed a stuttering stream of hot ComBloc lead at the charging cutthroats. With pinpoint deadly accuracy, as lead whined off the stone above their heads and thudded into the dead bodies around them, Eagle Force scythed down the enemy, driving New Conquistadors into each other with three-round bursts that blasted open chests, punched in faces, and exploded skulls. Blood, muck, gray brain matter, and shattered chunks of skull spattered the walls and added fresh gore to the carnage.

When the blaze of weapons fire ended, a hollow ring seemed to echo up and down the corridor. Gabriel saw McCoy crawl over the dead and the wounded prisoners.

Blood was pumping from the ragged hunk of red meat that was the DEA man's leg. Teeth gritted, he looked up at Gabriel. Not all of the prisoners, Gabriel noticed, had been slaughtered. Some had been wounded, and they gnashed their teeth, faces contorted in pain. And at the least six New Conquistadors were groaning, writhing in their own pools of steadily blossoming crimson. A second later, they scrabbled through their blood, clawing for AK-47s.

"Zac! Dutch! Cover the door!" Gabriel yelled.

As the two commandos covered their rear, Gabriel and Simms, stepping over the dead and the dying, swiftly advanced down the corridor. Gabriel heard the dry click from his AK-47 as he tried to squeeze off a burst. There was no time to snatch up a spare clip off the dead enemy and reload. And Gabriel heard Simms viciously curse his Russian assault rifle. It was time for some nose-to-nose, hand-to-hand vengeance, Gabriel knew, wound up as tight as a coiled spring with rage.

Three cutthroats rose from the dirt floor, caked in dust and blood. Hate and vengeance burning in their eyes, they lifted their AK-47s. But they never drew target acquisition.

Like some Viking berserkers, Gabriel and Simms swept over the enemy. Wielding their AK-47s like battle-axes, the ex-CIA assassin and the black commando drove the butts of their assault rifles through skullbone with savage, craning blows. The face of one enemy soldier seemed to implode into his brains as Gabriel drove his butt square into the guy's mouth and nose. Gabriel felt the enemy's entire face shatter like glass on the receiving end of his blow.

Simms lanced the steel-tipped toe of a combat boot through the temple of another of the Devil's cutthroats, who had appeared to rise from the dead.

His hand curling into a tiger claw, Gabriel ripped out the throat of another New Conquistador. The enemy soldier stood there, teetering on rubbery legs, staring at Gabriel for a second in shock and horror, then tumbled into the wall as the ex-CIA assassin let the bloody piece of flesh fall from his hand.

"C'mon, V.G.! We've gotta get outta here!" Dillinger called, flanking the doorway, the Dutchman peering around the corner.

Quickly, Gabriel and Simms hauled in a half-dozen spare clips each for the AK-47s. Gabriel then savored a moment of good luck. From two corpses, he plucked a total of five RGD-5 hand grenades. He crammed two of the four-and-a-half-inch Russian grenades into his pants pockets and handed Simms the other three grenades. Cracking home fresh thirty-round banana clips into their AK-47s, Gabriel and Simms began backpedaling toward Dillinger and Boolewarke.

McCoy braced his back against the wall, sat up. As he passed McCoy, Gabriel met the DEA man's burning gaze.

"Looks like you're out of the picture."

McCoy cursed Gabriel.

"Don't take it so hard, pal. Sit tight. We'll be back for you. You need any help with a tourniquet?" Gabriel asked, nodding at the agent's mangled leg.

"I think I can handle that," he growled bitterly.

"Vic, we've got to get the hell on the run," Boolewarke urged.

Gabriel and Simms passed out two clips each to Dillinger and Boolewarke, and the black commando gave the ex-P.I. and the Dutchman each an RGD-5 grenade.

Gabriel turned back to McCoy. Some of the prisoners, hands clamped over shoulder or leg wounds, blood spurting between splayed fingers, looked at the four commandos pointedly. Gabriel read the gratitude in their eyes. A heavy silence filled the corridor. Sometimes silence spoke louder than words—particularly the silence of death. And the silence of resurrection. These men had been dead. Now they had a chance to live again. It was moments like this, Gabriel reflected, that the fighting and the killing of a brutal, sadistic enemy were worth the sacrifice of his sweat and blood and pain.

"I suggest you check the dead to make sure they're just that," Gabriel told McCoy.

McCoy nodded that he understood. As Gabriel prepared to lead his commandos out of the cellblock, the DEA man called out. "Hey."

Gabriel turned. "Hey, what?"

McCoy drew a deep breath. The hardness in his eyes softened some. "I was here for six months. You've got no idea what these bastards have done to us, what we've been through."

"We got a taste of it," Gabriel said. "I can imagine the rest."

"I never thought I'd be going home. . . ."

"You're not home free yet," Gabriel said. "None of us are."

"Yeah, well, you've given me and the rest of these men some hope. Thanks, whoever you are."

"Take care of that leg," was Gabriel's parting shot.

Crouching beside the outside corner of the cellblock, Gabriel checked the clearing, then looked toward the temple. Eyelids narrowed to mere slits, he peered through the murk of dawn, listening intently for any telltale evidence of the enemy beyond. Gabriel heard only the howling and screeching of jungle wildlife, rising, it seemed, in a pitched fury, as if the monkeys and the exotic birds had sensed the murderous rage of man unleashed.

They had passed the bivouac on their way to the cellblock, and Gabriel was sure more New Conquistadors would have come running at the sound of weapons fire. Unless they were waiting in ambush in the darkness of the temple doorways. Gabriel didn't see any sign of the enemy.

With a wave of his hand, Gabriel led the commandos across the clearing. They had to keep moving, take the fight to the enemy.

Eagle Force spread out in a skirmish line, turning from side to side, checking their flanks and rear. Maybe the enemy had already come running from the camp and could now be counted among the dead in the prison corridor, Gabriel thought. Or maybe they had retreated toward the cocaine refinery. That made the most sense to Gabriel. The worst scenario Hernandez could envision would be the destruction of his refinery and his precious cocaine. If it looked as if there was an attack by an invading force, Gabriel believed that Hernandez would order the bulk of his mercenary army to seal off a perimeter around the refinery and fight to the last man. It went without saying, judging Hernandez for the savage that he was, that the Devil's coke was worth far more to him than the lives of his own men.

As he closed down on the temple, jogging toward a ten-foot statue of a bat god, Gabriel heard Simms call out.

"Vic! Take a look at this!"

Pivoting, his AK-47 poised to fire, Gabriel suddenly checked his trigger finger.

A group of six newly freed prisoners emerged from the shadows near the cellblock. Three New Conquistadors were being savagely beaten, fists and feet pummeling their faces and heads. As soon as those cutthroats hit the ground, they were hauled to their feet and further treated to a bitter taste of their own poison.

Eagle Force gathered near the foot of the temple steps. Grim-faced, they watched as the newly freed inmates kicked and punched their prisoners toward the pits.

Their voices shrill with terror, the New Conquistadors pleaded for mercy.

They found none.

"What do they say?" Simms asked. "Payback's a bitch?"

"And the bitch is demanding some right now," Dillinger added.

Desperately, a New Conquistador struggled to free himself from the clutches of his captors. He was slung into a pit. There was a dull splash. The shit pit, Gabriel knew.

"See no evil," Dillinger said, wiping some of the sweat off his forehead with the back of his hand.

Another cutthroat was tossed into the snake pit. A bone-chilling scream knifed the air.

"Hear no evil," growled Dillinger, AK-47 lowering by his side.

And, as the screams faded, a fresh voice of horror ripped into the steamy dawn air.

The last New Conquistador was picked up and dumped into the piranha pit.

"Speak no evil."

Gabriel turned away from the execution sight. The screams of a man being eaten alive by piranha filled his ears.

"Come on," he said, and led his commandos away from the statue of the bat god.

Symbol of death.

Gabriel put that horror behind him.

The grin held frozen, from all eternity and for all eternity, on the bat god's stone lips.

Gabriel found the Devil's camp deserted. He wasn't about -to trust first impressions, though. Quickly but thoroughly, he and his commandos checked each and every tent.

They found no cutthroats laying in ambush for them.

The sun had begun to clear the green mushroom heads of the jungle treeline. Already their fatigues were soaked with moisture. The air seemed to burn around Gabriel as he drew the steamy heat into his lungs. Sweat stinging into his eyes and burning into the cuts on his face like battery acid, he turned toward his commandos as they jogged up on him from the rear.

They hadn't managed to confiscate any weapons. But Boolewarke had found his Barnett Panzer crossbow. The recovery of his crossbow, given to him by his father, seemed to surge a new grim determination into the Dutchman's eyes. He even managed a grin.

"At least some of these bastards know a fine weapon when they see one," the Dutchman said. "Christ, I thought I'd lost it forever."

Dillinger spat. "Lucky you."

Boolewarke slapped the ex-P.I. on the back. "Cheer up, old man. You can always order a fresh pair of pearl-handled Colts. Me and this bow go back way before the Recces."

Again, Dillinger spat. "Like I said."

"Let's move it," Gabriel growled.

Swiftly, Gabriel led his commandos down the trail, heading in the direction of the last battlefront.

They still had a Devil to burn.

And Gabriel was determined to turn the heat up in the Colombian jungle. With hellfire.

Hernandez was cursing his troops for turning and running back to the refinery. The cowards! The four commandos had broken out of their cell and apparently freed the other prisoners. There was no doubt in his mind that the *mercenarios*, with their captured weapons, would attack his refinery. The report from his troops was in. And it was a grim message that they had to relay.

141

But they were only four men, after all. Still, he knew they were tough hombres, and they wouldn't just head for the river and leave their deadly business unfinished. No, they had come there to Fortress El Dorado to kill him and raze his refinery. He would see that his force fought down to the last man. Or he would start killing the cowards himself.

"Raul!" he barked at Pizarro, as the last twenty or so New Conquistadors gathered around the druglord. "Take your men, if that's what you call them, and go kill those cabrones! Do not come back here unless you have cut their heads off with your machete. *Comprende?*"

Pizarro cocked the bolt on his AK-47. He nodded.

The whole refinery seemed to have been thrown into a blind panic. Under the threat of death, Hernandez had ordered the chemists and the labor force to keep working. To make certain his labor force understood that he meant business, he had ordered the executions of three campesinos. The others got the message. They kept working. Four stinking *mercenarios* were not about to send him running like some dog with its tail tucked between its legs.

Then, as Pizarro began to lead his men toward the jungle trail, the grenade hit the ground in front of El Leon, bounced, and rolled into the middle of the amassed New Conquistadors.

Autofire suddenly blazed from the dense bushes of the jungle. A hail of lead tore into the heart of the New Conquistadors.

Cursing, seeing his worst nightmare boil up out of the gloom before his eyes, Hernandez belly flopped to the ground.

The grenade detonated.

Chapter 15

The fiery blast sent New Conquistadors whirling through the air like broken bowling pins. Countless serrated steel fragments sheared off flesh and ripped out eyes. As smoke drifted away from the carnage and severed limbs twirled away from the fireball, Eagle Force cut loose with their AK-47s. The commandos ended the agony for the New Conquistadors squirming in their gore with their hands slapped over blind eyes.

It was mop-up time, and Gabriel intended to burn the Devil's palace down to the ground. He wanted to leave nothing behind in that jungle hell but ashes and dust. And, of course, the broken, bloodied corpses of the enemy.

A finger of flame stabbed through the doorway behind Hernandez.

Gabriel pulled the pin on his second RGD-5 and hurled the deadly explosive.

"Noooooo!!!" Hernandez shrieked.

New Conquistadors were mowed down under the relentless barrage of Eagle Force lead. Slapping home fresh mags into their AK-47s, Boolewarke and Simms broke from cover. Firing on the run, they swept over any wounded enemy numbers, the Dutchman and the black commando triggering short bursts into the faces of their former captors. Dillinger held back on the trigger of his

AK-47, washing lead over any enemy numbers that vaulted to their feet, covering the advance of the Dutchman and Simms.

"Payback time, you fuckers!" Dillinger hollered, stitching lines of bullets up the spines of New Conquistadors.

An explosion pealed from the doorway of the cocaine refinery. The blast puked a fireball from the doorway, hurtling stone hunks, strips of mosquito netting, and bits and pieces of wet meat over Hernandez. The druglord hit the ground, covered his head with his arms.

Boolewarke and Simms ran past Hernandez. They crouched beside the smoking hole. Bullets screamed off the jagged stone above their heads. Together, Boolewarke and Simms pulled the pins on their grenades. They looked at each other and nodded. Then they tossed the grenades through the swirling smoke. As the twin blasts rumbled beyond them, men screaming as lethal steel fragments tore them to shreds, the Dutchman and the black commando bolted into the cocaine refinery.

They found the refinery a scene of utter chaos. Everywhere, Boolewarke and Simms saw figures bolting for exits in the far corners, beating a hasty retreat from the merchants of death. Most of those men fleeing for their lives were weaponless. Four men were armed with AK-47s.

As lead spat toward their positions, Boolewarke and Simms triggered their AK-47s on full-auto slaughter. New Conquistadors spun, bloody rag dolls, down the length of a long table. Fist-sized holes in their chests gouting blood, they bowled down large glass containers of ether. Savagely, Boolewarke and Dillinger raked those cutthroats with an extended burst of death messages. From the far corner of the refinery, a fire blazed to life.

"Looks like the Devil's house is about to go up in flames, Johnny!" Boolewarke yelled.

"Let's beat feet, Dutchie! Looks like the Devil's finally about to find his real hell."

Outside, Gabriel loomed over Fernando Hernandez. He pointed his AK-47 at the druglord's face. Defiant hatred stared back up at Gabriel. Blood ran down El Diablo's face from where steel fragments had sliced open furrows in his forehead.

"Go ahead, cabron," Hernandez hissed. "Kill me."

Gabriel hesitated.

"Kill me!" the druglord screamed.

Gabriel felt his trigger finger tighten up. Damn, but he wanted to blast the hate right off the druglord's face with a quick burst. After all the suffering, all the misery this scum had caused . . .

Then Gabriel's eyes fell on something. Beside Hernandez laid a silver Ronson lighter. Gabriel decided to find out just how much the druglord's life meant to him. Turning, Gabriel saw the rows of coca leaves, stretched out on the nets between trees nearby. The rows seemed to go on for at least a quarter-mile. El Dorado's gold.

Then, out of the corner of his eye, Gabriel spotted the huge figure charging him, the machete poised to split his skull open. Gabriel flung himself at Pizarro's knees. El Leon flipped over Gabriel, slammed to the ground beside his master.

Leaping to his feet, Gabriel triggered his AK-47. At that same instant, three other AK-47s erupted to pump a fusillade of ComBloc lead into Pizarro. Eagle Force made Pizarro dance a long jig of death. They ventilated the Lion with a fusillade of ComBloc lead. Even still, Pizarro lifted his machete, chunks of cloth and flesh shearing off his massive frame from 7.62mm lead, and took a step toward Gabriel. Three rounds then burst through the back of Pizarro's skull. Gabriel drilled Pizarro in the chest with a three-round burst as the cutthroat's head shattered like an eggshell. Drenched in his own spewing gore, Pizarro dropped.

Hernandez just laid on the ground in shocked silence.

"What about the others who ran out?" Boolewarke wanted to know as he and Simms moved away from the rubble around the entrance to the refinery.

"If they didn't have any weapons," Gabriel said, moving toward Hernandez, "let 'em go. I'd say the chemists and the work force have just fled into the jungle. If they came here willingly, then maybe the jungle will take care of them for us."

Gabriel rested a grim stare on Hernandez. "It's over, Hernandez. Your nightmare gold is about to go up in smoke."

"What are you going to do?"

"It's not what I'm going to do, it's what you're going to do," Gabriel told Hernandez. "After that, your fate is out of my hands."

Hernandez looked up at Gabriel in fear and confusion.

Gabriel picked up the lighter, dropped it on the druglord's chest. "Do what I tell you right now, and I won't kill you. *I* won't. But I know there are some men back down the trail who'd like to have a few words with you. If I remember correctly," he lied to the druglord, "I think I heard something back there about snake chow."

"What is it you want me to do?"

"Put the torch to your coca leaves, then burn down your own damn house."

Hernandez hesitated. Gabriel saw the wheels spinning in the druglord's eyes. No, he didn't want to do it. Not one bit. So Gabriel pointed his AK-47 at the druglord's face.

"Well?"

Hernandez spat. He picked up the lighter.

Epilogue

Slowly, weapons low by their sides, Eagle Force walked around the ancient temple. As he headed away from the bat god, Gabriel saw the surviving prisoners of Fortress El Dorado moving toward him. At first they moved like wooden figures. But the mere sight of Hernandez seemed to spark fire in their eyes.

Gabriel shoved Hernandez to the ground. Under the threat of death, the druglord had torched his kingdom. As he had watched his "gold" burn before his eyes, the life had seemed to wilt right out of Hernandez. As the coca leaves and his refinery burned, he had said nothing. Instead, the druglord had wept. Bitterly. It was a sight that had made Gabriel want to crush the guy right into the ground beneath the heel of his boot. But Gabriel knew there were others who had probably earned that right more than he had.

The sun burned down on the jungle clearing from a cobalt sky. In the distance, behind Gabriel and his commandos, palls of thick black smoke boiled over the treeline. The jungle trees shuddered with the weight of squirrel monkeys. A brightly colored wild bird soared over the temple.

Exhausted, his body stiff, sore, and aching from head to toe, Gabriel sucked in a deep breath. Suddenly he heard a voice inside his head. It was a voice long since gone.

The voice of the dead. A voice that had been buried beneath the crushing weight of the insanity savages like Fernando Hernandez exported.

Dillinger canted his AK-47 to his shoulder.

Simms spat on the ground.

The Barnett Panzer crossbow was once again slung around Boolewarke's shoulder.

Gabriel searched the gaunt faces of the newly freed prisoners. With hatred, they looked at Hernandez. No longer did the druglord seem so arrogant. No longer did El Diablo look so powerful. Like some worm, Hernandez tried to crawl away from the clutches of the men he had tortured and beaten for so long.

It was no use.

Vengeance, Vic Gabriel was again witnessing, was one of the most powerful motivating forces in the human spirit.

Hernandez screamed. As he was hauled to his feet and shoved toward the pits, he looked back at Gabriel in terror.

"Why? Why did you do this?" the druglord wailed.

Gabriel turned away as the free men flung Fernando Hernandez into the piranha pit.

The screams seemed to lash at Gabriel's backside from a mile away.

"Because," Gabriel muttered to himself, feeling the pain of terrible memories burn up from the core of his soul. "Because . . . I had a brother."

TERROR AT 37,000 FEET

Flight 666 has been hijacked by a bloodthirsty band of Iranian terrorists . . . and they're starting to execute the passengers. The world is helpless to save them, so it's up to the men of Eagle Force to blast the kill-crazy fanatics into the waiting arms of Allah!

Here's an exciting preview of Book #3 in Dan Schmidt's EAGLE FORCE series:

FLIGHT
666

They're coming at you!
Look for Eagle Force
wherever Bantam Books are sold.

The Arab felt the first few beads of sweat dampen his brow. Knowing the time was near, he felt his heart pounding in his chest like a jackhammer, and he ran his tongue over lips dried from nervous tension. He was nervous, all right, and with good reason. Within minutes, he was about to shape the destiny of two hundred people. Change their lives forever. Bind their lives together in blood and terror.

A little more than an hour ago Flight 666 had departed from the Paris international airport. Now the Boeing 727 was thirty-seven thousand feet in the air, soaring like some great bird above a sea of white billowy clouds, heading east for its destination, Tel Aviv, the infidel city of the hated Jew.

He stared out the window, squinting. The sun blazed in the east, burning over the clouds like some blinding beacon greeting the day, and it hurt his eyes to look out the window for more than a few seconds. The sun, a huge orange fireball, he thought, gaze narrowed, as he peered off into the horizon. *But a black sun is about to set over the enemies of Iran and the brave and great Shiite peoples of my homeland.*

There were at least two hundred passengers aboard Flight 666, he figured. And he wondered how many Jews and how many Americans were aboard the flight. Everything had been worked out, down to the last detail. Weapons had been smuggled aboard by French freedom fighters, cargo workers who had been planted in the mainstream of employment at the airport eight months ago. Preparation and proper planning were the keys. The French had gone soft, he thought, after being trampled in the dust by the great Jew killers during World War II. France had provided the perfect springboard for his plan.

Irzhim Mouhbami looked across the aisle at his three fellow combatants in the war against the Great Satan. He nodded.

It was time.

A ball of sweat broke from Mouhbami's forehead, burned into his eyes.

"Excuse me, sir."

Mouhbami looked at the flight attendant. She was blond, and very pretty. Flawless features, flawless complexion. Perhaps there would be a few moments when . . . No. He pushed the thought aside. He had Allah's work to do.

"Would you like something to drink?"

Mouhbami smiled. "A glass of ice water. Thank you."

The smile melted from Irzhim Mouhbami's lips. He watched the pretty flight attendant, a Western slut, he thought, move up to the next row of seats as a fellow warrior in the battle against the Great Satan walked to the lavatory.

Vic Gabriel didn't like commercial airline flights. An ex–Green Beret who had always demanded of himself that he be in charge of his own destiny and in control of the environment around him, he had a problem with entrusting his life to a pilot he had never met before. At the moment, his life and the lives of at least two hundred other people aboard Air France Flight 666 were in the hands of a disembodied voice over the intercom, he thought. He was beginning to regret his decision to take this offbeat assignment for Sweitzer and Eisen Enterprises, a European-based conglomerate, but a conglomerate of what he wasn't exactly certain.

Vic Gabriel also had another fear about commercial airline flights.

The fear of skyjacking. The fear of being unarmed, as he was right then, his life balanced in the equation of the Great Void by a suicidal maniac who had no regard for human life. Was he being paranoid? Was his imagination working overtime with unjustified fears? He didn't think so. After four brutal missions with his team of crack commandos of Eagle Force, Vic Gabriel knew that anything at any time was possible. And he also knew from grim experience that to survive in the soldier-for-hire trade, a warrior had to expect the unexpected, and be prepared for anything.

At the moment, sitting by the window in the third-to-last row, his two employers next to him, all he could do, or should do, he decided, was ride out the flight and get some rest. His other three commandos of Eagle Force were back at Eagle's Nest Citadel in the Pyrenees of southern France, soaking up some much-deserved R&R, while he was bound for Israel, tackling a stint as a bodyguard for Al Sweitzer and Peter Eisen, businessmen. Rubbing his jaw, Gabriel looked at Sweitzer and Eisen. He recalled that day, almost a week ago, when they had come to him at Eagle's Nest Citadel and offered him the assignment. They had claimed they were in the import-export business, but exactly what they imported or exported didn't come up on the computers at the citadel. Gabriel had pressed the two Jewish businessmen, and they had vaguely alluded to arms dealing. They didn't look like weapons smugglers to Gabriel. They were small of stature, with bland, almost nondescript features. Pale skin, soft hands, both of them wearing glasses. No, they looked more like bankers than gunrunners.

"Do you have any questions regarding your assignment, Gabriel?"

Gabriel looked at Eisen, then the flight attendant asked them if they cared for any beverages. Gabriel waited for Eisen and Sweitzer to order some iced tea, and he ordered the same.

"Questions," the ex–Special Forces warrior grunted. "You two seem damn reluctant to answer any questions. All I know is that I'm suppose to follow you two around Israel and make sure you don't get blown away. My gut feeling is telling me there's more to this than you're willing to let on. A safe bet is that you're running guns to some Israeli terrorist movement."

"Sssshh!" Eisen hissed, his hard, beady eyes looking over at the next aisle. "Keep your voice down."

Sweitzer leaned forward, looking across Eisen. "You're being paid fifty thousand dollars, Mr. Gabriel, for a two-month assignment. Paid not to ask a lot of questions; that was the agreement we made back in France."

And so it was, Gabriel recalled. These two had answered the ad Eagle Force had placed in the well-known, controversial French mercenary magazine, *Le Mercenaire*.

Gabriel spread his hands.

"Hey, you asked if I had any questions."

"We expected," Eisen said, again looking around at the other passengers in the aisle across from him, "a little tact on your part. Not for you to be hypothesizing about what we are out loud for everyone aboard this airliner to hear."

"You're not being paranoid, are you, friend?" Gabriel asked. "Now, you did mention something about my being helpful with military tactics. What exactly did you mean by that?"

Sweitzer heaved a sigh. "I would've felt much more comfortable, sir, if you had allowed us to take accommodations in first class."

"Couldn't do it," Gabriel answered. "I hate commercial airline flights. Never take them, if I can help it. I like to be able to keep my eyes on what's going on around me."

Suddenly Sweitzer was peering over the head of his seat. He looked at his partner, then at Gabriel. In a low, conspiratorial voice he said, "Have you noticed those four Arab-looking types in the back, Gabriel?"

Gabriel looked. Just then, he saw one of the Arab-looking men rise from his seat and move toward the lavatory. Yes, he had noticed the man and three other men who looked like Arabs the minute they had boarded. They were unsavory-looking characters, he had decided. And if ever someone looked like a hijacker...

"What about them?"

"They smell Arab to me," Sweitzer said.

"So?"

"So?" Sweitzer grunted. "They could be terrorists, planning to hijack this plane. Then what of us?"

"If they do, they do," Gabriel said with more confidence than he felt. "There's two hundred people or more aboard, Sweitzer. I hope you're just as concerned for them in the event of a hijacking."

"Are you implying that I am without feeling for my fellowman?"

Gabriel shrugged, and a look of contempt flickered through Sweitzer's eyes.

Eisen elaborated on Sweitzer's statement. "We are Jews, Mr. Gabriel. We have much more to fear from Arab terrorists than you."

"Camel dung," Gabriel quietly growled. "Terrorists don't discriminate about who they kill."

"Just the same, you are being paid to protect us," Eisen said. "Keep an eye on them, if you don't mind."

Gabriel looked over his seat again. He met the eyes of one of the Arabs. Cold, empty eyes. He sensed something deadly about the man. And a strange smile slid over the Arab's lips.

Warning bells klaxoned in Gabriel's head.

The Arab rose from his seat.

Why he knew it was going to happen, he wasn't sure, but Vic Gabriel became a trapped spectator in his own worst nightmare.

Oh, Christ, he thought. *It can't be....*

The Arab who had stepped into the lavatory opened the door as the flight attendant prepared the food-and-beverage cart.

With a vicious backhand, the Arab knocked the flight attendant over the cart, spilling drinks and creating a racket that alerted the passengers all the way up the aisle. Cursing, screaming, he held up a hand grenade, threw three pistols to his three companions in the back. Instantly, the four Arabs were moving up the aisle.

"Nobody move! Nobody move, or you all die! This is a hijacking!"

Shrill screams pierced the air.

One of the Arabs belted a woman in the mouth with the butt of his pistol.

"You all die! You all die!"

Vic Gabriel's worst-case scenario became his ultimate nightmarish reality. Weaponless, he felt frozen in some void between life and death, a puppet dangling by a string over an open fire. Even though he'd never been dead and gone to the beyond, he sure as hell at that moment felt worse than dead. He was helpless, and he couldn't remember when he'd ever felt so incapable of controlling an environment of terror. For a warrior with countless campaigns of death behind him, this inability to deal with just such a scenario was inexcusable, and he felt small, weak, vulnerable. The terrorists had moved quick, too quick for him to even jump one of them and make some suicidal grandstand play. But the more he thought about it, the more he knew he wouldn't have physically confronted the four heavily armed madmen now completely in control of the situation. Suicide was a fool's bargain, usually done in an insane moment of despair over sins or crimes committed for which he couldn't, or didn't want to pay for. Gabriel knew the smartest thing he could do was to wait, bide his time, look for an opening, and seize the moment.

There were others who couldn't wait for that moment to arrive.

"No!" Sweitzer screamed. The Jewish businessman leaped to his feet, clawing at one of the terrorists. Snarling, that terrorist belted Sweitzer in the side of his face. The sight on the gun barrel sliced open a deep gash on Sweitzer's cheek. Blood flowing down the side of his face, Sweitzer was propelled by the blow back into his seat. Clutching at his face, he screamed an obscenity through his hands. For long moments, as two of the Arab's comrades slid up the aisle, waving their guns and threatening to kill everybody by detonating the grenade, the terrorist held his gun, aimed rock-steady, inches from Sweitzer's face.

"Give me one reason why I should not kill you now!" the terrorist screamed. "One reason!"

Feeling grim, but summoning up some kind of twisted courage in the face of death, Gabriel looked at the terrorist, cracked, "Because he gives ten grand a year in charity to the PLO."

The terrorist didn't know how to take that. For the briefest of moments, Vic Gabriel was sure the Arab was going to cut him down in cold blood. Then the terrorist took a step back. He showed Gabriel a lopsided grin.

"You are either very brave or very foolish to talk to Irzhim Mouhbami like that."

Gabriel knew it, damn but he knew it. Adrenaline

was burning so fast and furious through him that the ex-Special Forces warrior heard his heart thumping in his ears. But one thing he knew a fanatic respected was courage, even reckless, suicidal courage. The fanatic gave ground, nodded, as if he understood something about Gabriel.

Mouhbami turned. "Brother Karij," he barked at the Arab behind him. His gaze steely, he leveled that stare, filled with hate, directly on Gabriel. "Watch these three. I do not like them already. I do not trust them. If they move an inch, shoot them. This one here," he said, waving his gun at Gabriel, "he has the look of a soldier, and he has the voice of a man not afraid of death. Watch him as if you were guarding your home from a poisonous snake." The lopsided grin again. "I go now to the cockpit to have a word with our esteemed captain." He nodded curtly at Gabriel. "Enjoy the flight."

Marching several steps backward, gun still trained on Gabriel, Irzhim Mouhbami made his way to the cockpit.

The Arab with the hand grenade was still cursing and threatening to blow the jumbo jet into paradise.

"What a sweetheart, huh, fellas," Gabriel hissed under his breath. The brutal sounds of fists thudding bone and open palms cracking flesh reached Gabriel's ears as the terrorists silenced screams of terror with violence.

Eisen and Sweitzer stared at Gabriel with astonishment.

"You are taking this mighty lightly, Mr. Gabriel," Eisen rasped. "I can't say I appreciate your cavalier attitude."

"I'm taking this about as lightly as stepping onto a mine field, friend. Don't forget, I've got fifty grand invested in you two."

Sweitzer was visibly shaken. He groaned, and his face fell into his hands. "Is that all our lives are worth to you—money? Perhaps I should have expected nothing less from a common mercenary."

"Right now, friend, none of our lives are worth a common turd."

"This is your captain. I want everyone to remain calm and do as you are told, and I have their solemn word you will not be harmed in any way."

Bullshit, Cap'n. Vic Gabriel wished he could snatch the pilot through the intercom and slap him silly, back into reality. The guy was putting up a front, a false front, one that could well crumble down on the heads of innocent victims. Vic Gabriel wanted to know exactly who *they* were, because if he got the chance, he was going to grind these fanatics up into raw hamburger meat with his bare hands and kick them out the plane as human garbage for the dung heap in their Allah's paradise.

"We have been hijacked by terrorists of the Iranian Revolutionary Front. . . ."

Gabriel heard the sharp guttural groan as Mouhbami cracked the pilot over the head with gunmetal.

"No, no, no," Sweitzer blubbered to himself, "this can't be happening . . . this can't be . . ."

Brother Karij appeared beside Sweitzer so swiftly, it seemed as if he had materialized out of thin air. "Shut up," he hissed, and piledrived his fist into Sweitzer's jaw. Recoiling, riding the blow back into his seat, Sweitzer started to rise, but the Arab thrust his gun into the bleeding face.

"Do it! Stand! Do it!"

Gabriel saw the naked terror etched on the faces of the passengers across the aisle. The other two terrorists had positioned themselves strategically up the aisle. Like cornered animals, their heads constantly moved from side to side, their bodies swiveling, gunmetal searching for any who felt inclined to mutiny against their insane authority. No one moved.

Gabriel noticed the guns were snub-nosed .38s, easy to smuggle aboard the aircraft and conceal in the john. The grenade, which was held up in the air by the terrorist in the far front of the aircraft, looked like a Soviet F1. An impotent rage remained lodged in the soldier's bowels. There was no doubt in Vic Gabriel's mind that these fanatics would blow the plane up if their demands were not met, whatever those demands were.

The voice of Irzhim Mouhbami boomed over the intercom. This seemed to keep brother Karij from extracting any more blood from Sweitzer.

"This is Irzhim Mouhbami, soldier of the Iranian Revolutionary Front, fighting for the freedom of all Shiite Iranians in the face of Western imperialist oppression and aggression. The esteemed captain of this vessel of pig dogs and droppings of the Great Satan is wrong, gravely wrong. I have given no word, solemn or otherwise, as to my intentions. I am demanding the release of four hundred of our brothers in the fight for freedom from jails in Israel and Europe, where they are being wrongly imprisoned. We will be stopping in Athens, as scheduled, for refueling. If they refuse to let us land . . . I need not tell you what will happen. Then . . . we will be flying on to Iran. Again, I need not tell you what will happen if our final demands are not met. Death to infidels is my only solemn word."

Gabriel heard the groans of defeat and despair, sounds that seemed to echo and linger in the air of terror. Iran. Great, he thought. A big bird, baking in the sun of the Iranian desert, while fanatics made a circus out of terror, and, he guessed, a carnival out of death. Gabriel envisioned the media sharpening their pencils already. If they landed in Iran, Gabriel knew they could be grounded and trapped there for a long time. Months. Maybe years. He thought about Johnny Simms, Zac Dillinger and Henry van Boolewarke. He wondered how his commandos would take the news of this skyjacking. He knew how. And he suspected what they would do would be to load up for some Persian headhunting. If the fanatics let him live, Vic thought, they would wish they hadn't. Bet your ass on it.

"In just several moments," Mouhbami went on, "we will be collecting passports. All Jews, and any American citizens of the Great Satan aboard this vessel, will be dealt with accordingly. That is all. Prepare your passports." A chuckle rumbled over the intercom. "Enjoy your flight."

Gabriel looked at Eisen and Sweitzer. The two Jews seemed to shrink up into themselves with renewed fear. They looked at Gabriel with what he thought was pure hate. As if he was to blame for the predicament of the passengers. Now he felt as if he had to deal with more than just four enemies.

Vic Gabriel muttered a curse under his breath.

Flight 666, he thought, had become the devil's bargaining chip.

THRILLERS

Gripping suspense . . . explosive action . . . dynamic characters
. . . international settings . . . these are the elements that make for
great thrillers. Books guaranteed to keep you riveted to your seat.

Robert Ludlum:

☐ 28179	TREVAYNE	$5.95
☐ 27800	THE ICARUS AGENDA	$5.95
☐ 26256	THE AQUITAINE PROGRESSION	$5.95
☐ 26011	THE BOURNE IDENTITY	$5.95
☐ 26094	THE CHANCELLOR MANUSCRIPT	$5.95
☐ 26019	THE HOLCROFT COVENANT	$5.95
☐ 25899	THE MATARESE CIRCLE	$5.95
☐ 26430	THE OSTERMAN WEEKEND	$5.95
☐ 25270	THE PARSIFAL MOSAIC	$5.95
☐ 27109	THE ROAD TO GANDOLFO	$5.95
☐ 27146	THE SCARLATTI INHERITANCE	$5.95
☐ 26322	THE BOURNE SUPREMACY	$5.95

Frederick Forsyth:

☐ 05361	THE NEGOTIATOR	$19.95
☐ 25113	THE FOURTH PROTOCOL	$4.95
☐ 27673	NO COMEBACKS	$4.95
☐ 26630	DAY OF THE JACKAL	$4.95
☐ 26490	THE DEVIL'S ALTERNATIVE	$4.95
☐ 26846	THE DOGS OF WAR	$4.95
☐ 27198	THE ODESSA FILE	$4.95

Prices and availability subject to change without notice.

Buy them at your local bookstore or use this page to order.

- -

Bantam Books, Dept. TH, 414 East Golf Road, Des Plaines, IL 60016

Please send me the books I have checked above. I am enclosing $_____
(please add $2.00 to cover postage and handling). Send check or money order
—no cash or C.O.D.s please.

Mr/Ms _____

Address _____

City/State _____ Zip _____

TH—9/89

Please allow four to six weeks for delivery.